I0567609

Volume I

TY HANSON

Copyright © 2022 Ty Hanson

All rights reserved

This is a work of fiction. The characters, names, places, and events portrayed in this book are fictitious. Any similarity to real persons, living or dead, events or locales is coincidental and not intended by the author.

No part of this book may be reproduced, or stored in a retrieval system, or transmitted in any form or by any means, electronic, mechanical, photocopying, recording, or otherwise, without express written permission of the author.
For more information, address: finchzero@gmail.com

ISBN 978-0-646-86320-7 (paperback)

Cover Art: Elmer Damaso
Character art: Hary Istiyoso
Environment art: Jordan Grimmer
Editor: Jan-Andrew Henderson
Proofreader / Editor: Mighty Writing Co.

www.millenniumexile.com

To all who have supported

the Millennium Exile project over the years,

I promised that I'd never give up.

To my loving wife,

*Thank you for always being there, and for loving me
through all my nonsense.*

To those who didn't believe,

Who in the hell do you think I am?

This book is for all the dreamers of the world.

*Aim high, don't be afraid of failure and most
importantly...*

Stay true to yourself.

*"Don't aim to break the glass ceiling; aim to shatter
it."*

– Matshona Dhliwayo

THE TWILIGHT FOREST

AVALON

DEVI
ISL

FEL BARA

THE JAGGED
WASTELANDS

ENDERS

KOR

FLEECE

TEMPLIN

SOMA

THE
S

REMNAN
ISLANDS

VEN'S
EAK

THE SHATTERED PENINSULA

TRIFFICA
ISLANDS

XERXES

KETHLAR

THE VEGA
CITADEL

THE VORPAL
PLAINS

KURAU

FLAGSTONE

RYUUGA

SALACE

AUSTRAL

KANSINGTON

GREENFIRE
VALLEY

LIFON

CHEDDA

BRIZDEN

ANGEL'S
COVE

VENTRIS

PULSE

KOU

Welcome to Ryner.

A planet that has flourished amidst three great nations: The Republic of Kou, East Londell, and The Kingdom of Mane.

From the icy heights of the Shattered Peninsula; to the green pastures of Fleece, Kou is filled with impossibly beautiful landscapes, mythical creatures, and unique plant life. Yet despite its beautiful veneer, Kou has a dark and tumultuous history that has long since been lost to the passages of time.

Now, on the continents of Fel-Bara and Xerxes, another story unfolds, one that will decide the fate of all who live on Ryner.

Mission One:

GRAVE

Chapter One

The ground shook violently, and rock shattered, laying waste to entire mountains and landscapes as two unknown figures of tremendous power fought one another. One was a man, clad heavily in a mysterious black armor, while the other appeared far more demonic. A pair of giant wings stretched from his back, razor-sharp horns protruded from above his elven ears; and two whip-like tails hung from beneath his long, blue-green hair.

The armored warrior pushed back his devilish foe in a show of unparalleled strength. However, just before he could land the finishing blow, thousands of tortured screams filled the man's head, pleading for mercy. He dropped to one knee, disorientated, and clutching at his face. His mysterious armor began to stir—resonating with his distress. It swirled across his body and began to bubble. The demon slowly backed away as a dark, menacing energy filled the atmosphere.

Suddenly, several black tendrils sprouted from the armor and burrowed deep into the ground, lifting the warrior high into the air as if he were being sacrificed.

He screamed as the armor began to swell, and a large crack snapped across his helmet, revealing a single green eye—open wide in confusion and panic.

***

"Vincent, Vincent…VINCENT!"

A young man woke suddenly, his golden eyes shooting open. Sitting up quickly, his tattered baseball cap fell from his face. He had an athletic build and wore a black singlet, long pants, and dirty sneakers. As he put his hat back on to manage his long, unkempt, purple hair, the young man looked up to see four disheveled children standing over him with panicked looks on their grimy faces.

"What the hell?" Vincent growled, "how many times do I hafta tell you, kids, not to wake me like that!?" Beads of sweat ran down his face as he caught his breath, recovering from the strange dream.

Vincent had these nightmares regularly—an assortment of visions showing himself in the body of another young warrior amidst a time of war and chaos.

Three of the children recoiled from the scolding, but the fourth stood his ground, determined. "The Vipers are causing trouble again! They're barging into everyone's houses and stealin' food!"

"That so?" Vincent questioned lightly, scratching his head. "Here I was thinking you kids were botherin' me bout some crap like, *Oh Vincent, jump really high with us on your back*, or *Waahhh, can you get my ball down from that high roof?*"

He stood up in the shady back alley where he had been sleeping and dusted himself off. "But a good ol' fight with the Vipers is just what I needed to cure some of my boredom," he smiled broadly.

"Actually, I haven't heard from them for a while…but I guess that lot will never learn."

"This time, they've got more guys with 'em, and I'm pretty sure it's in case you show up!" the determined child said with urgency.

"Y-yeah, it's a huuuge group…way bigger than normal!" interjected another.

Vincent chuckled at this thought, amused that the Vipers would try and prepare for him. "That's okay, just gives me more of a workout, is all." He stretched his limbs.

"One thing I need to know, though," Vincent asked with a serious gleam in his eyes. "Has anyone been hurt yet?"

"I don't know everything," the determined child answered quickly, "but they've roughed up a buncha people."

"Well, for what it's worth, you did a good job finding me…although it looks like you were followed." Vincent pointed to the end of the alleyway behind the children, where a hooded stranger loomed in the shadows.

As the man approached, flicking a knife between his fingers, Vincent stepped forward unphased. He held his right shoulder with his left hand while winding his right arm around to stretch his muscles. Cracking his neck sharply from side to side, he noticed the tattoo of a snake on the intruder's forearm—the tell-tale mark of the Vipers.

Despite his nonchalant attitude in such a dangerous situation, Vincent was distracted by a painful and almost crippling headache that often set in whenever he had these dreams.

The stranger grinned evilly and began to utter something, but before a full letter's sound could leave his lips, a heavy THWACK echoed throughout the alleyway. The aggressor's head bounced off the wall to his right, and his unconscious body fell to the floor.

Vincent stepped over the man's body, barely breaking stride, and threw the knife into a dumpster on his way past.

"Stay here until I get back," Vincent instructed.

"You'll be safe."

"Stay here?" one of the timid children stammered. "What if this guy wakes up? What do you expect *us* to do?"

Vincent chuckled and looked over his shoulder, the shadow of the brim of his hat hiding all but an amused smirk.

"Don't worry, he's not wakin' up for at least a few hours. I'll be back before the sun goes down," he said before walking down the alleyway and out of sight.

One of the children looked up to the sky. "But…the sun has already started to set. It'll be night soon."

"This is your first time meeting him cuz you're younger than us," the determined child said with his hands on his hips, "but Vincent's awesome! If he says we're safe here, then we are."

He looked down and playfully pushed the unconscious Viper's cheek around with the toe of his ragged shoe.

***

Nearby, fearful residents retreated to the corners of

their homes, huddled together, as members of the Viper gang rummaged through what little belongings they had. Around forty in number, they patrolled the ghettos, conducting home invasions in groups of six. Having benefitted from their numerous crimes, these men ate well. As a result, they had healthier physiques than the other desperate residents.

In the open main street, several women and children had been restrained and forced to their knees as members of the Vipers threatened them with bats, pipes, and assorted makeshift, weapons.

A heavily scarred man, wearing a sleeveless black jacket and brandishing a large sword, flicked a discarded cigarette into the air. Following its arc, he spotted Vincent standing on the rooftop above.

"What have you done this time, Badou?!" Vincent questioned angrily.

Vincent had known Badou for as long as he could remember. He used to look up to Badou when they were both kids. However, despite Vincent's best intentions, Badou always rejected him—just as everyone did.

Badou knew that Vincent would come to save the same people who hated him; their eyes widened in fear wherever he went. But even though they refused to accept him, Vincent continued to help them all the same. He could never turn his back on someone in need. All Vincent ever wanted was to help…to be a hero like his late father. While it pained him, Vincent was used to being hated.

"Knew you'd be along eventually, *Mr. Hero*," Badou said with scorn. He stretched his arms outward, showing off his large, muscular physique and looking pleased with himself. "You see, this time, I assured my victory!"

Vincent raised an eyebrow, distracted by his headache and confused by Badou's ridiculous claim. "Awww, look at you with your wittle plans!"

Despite Vincent's blasé attitude, Badou's smile grew.

"You've been screwing with us for years now. Hell, I can't even count how many of these scars are from you." Badou barked as he held open his jacket to reveal his bare chest. "But it got me thinking…if you've been getting in *my* way, you've probably been pissing off the other gangs too. Am I right?"

"Probably," Vincent nodded, trying to put together Badou's train of thought.

"So, me and the boys reached out to the other delinquent groups: The Four Horsemen, Paradise of Despair, and the Red Dragons. All of us are rivals from all over this shit-heap, but ya know what? Despite *all* our differences, the one thing we could agree on is you. You've been interfering with our business Vinny, and it's time we put you in the dirt once and for all!"

Vincent sucked his teeth, the underside of his tongue peaking through.

While he was usually confident in his abilities, the sheer number of hostages concerned him. He was disgusted that innocent people were being used as human shields, but he refused to give Badou the satisfaction of seeing how vulnerable it made him feel.

"You're tellin' me that with *all that* manpower, you *still* need to take women and children hostage?" Vincent crossed his arms. "That lack of confidence makes you look weak!"

Badou snapped his fingers, and a nearby thug grabbed one of the children, dragging him up by the hair and holding a jagged knife to his throat.

Then, in a moment that appeared to make time stand still, the man with the blade was kicked into the wall behind him, Vincent's foot firmly planted in his chest. His golden eyes were wild with anger and fixed on Badou as he descended.

The child fell to the ground, unhurt, and scrambled away, crying in fear.

The other hostages were quickly pulled backward, weapons held against their flesh. Vincent surveyed his surroundings. The hostages were too far from one another. There was no way that he could beat a group of this size without endangering innocent lives.

He slowly rose to his feet, holding up his arms in surrender. Despite the seemingly hopeless situation, Vincent was almost amused.

"Okay, ya got me," he exclaimed. "You really thought this one through, didn't ya, Doey-boy?"

Badou stepped forward, dragging his sword along the

concrete until he was almost nose-to-nose with Vincent.

"And yet, you *still* couldn't help yourself," he sneered. "You just had to dive in and attack the moment you got angry, didn't ya? You know, that temper of yours is what makes you predictable."

Vincent raised his head slightly. "And yet, you've never beaten me. Funny how being predictable means nothin' if you're strong."

Badou laughed loudly.

Stepping back into the street he raised his sword, twirling them on the spot, "Whaddya think all this is for?" he gestured to the scene before Vincent.

"Wow. It took you this long to finally come up with a plan to catch me? I'm not sure whether to be proud or just feel sorry for ya!"

Vincent was getting bored. He knew Badou was trying to get a rise out of him. He'd been in worse scrapes than this, and his strength had never failed him, so why would this time be any different?

Badou's smile faded to a scowl as he snapped his fingers again. "Take him."

Several thugs swarmed over to restrain Vincent. However, regardless of their numbers, they couldn't move him an inch.

"Let's get this straight. I come with you, and all of this stops right now?" Vincent asked, gesturing toward the hostages and ransacked buildings. A large man hung from his wrist while Vincent effortlessly swung him about.

Badou turned his back to Vincent and placed his hands on his hips, emphasizing dominance.

"You ain't really in a position to make demands here, so whaddya gonna do if we keep going? Huh?"

Vincent shrugged. "If you can't guarantee everyone's safety and return their belongings, I might as well take you all out right now," Vincent replied confidently.

Though he didn't know any of the hostages too well, he often protected everyone who lived in the ghettos from these large, violent gangs. Vincent could beat them in the blink of an eye if he wanted—but, this would require more force than he was comfortable exerting without endangering lives.

Badou turned back.

"You think we need any of the shit these filthy rats have?" he closed the distance between them and whispered in Vincent's ear. "We raided another district three days ago while you were busy rebuilding that house that burned down last week."

Vincent's eyes widened, realizing that the group had been distracting him and feeding off his absence elsewhere.

"That's right," Badou gloated. "We're the ones who started that fire. We knew that the mighty hero of the Ryuuga Ghetto would come and lend a hand. Haven't ya wondered why you hadn't seen us lately? What? Do you think that the big bad Vincent Clyne had scared us off? We've been staging these little 'accidents' for weeks now. When you go to help, we take advantage someplace else. Our food supplies are *so* full these days that I might just throw some out...just for the hell of it."

Badou's toothy grin widened.

"We got what we wanted from this little excursion, so move your ass!"

Vincent went quiet. His blood was boiling, and his muscles tightened with rage. He turned his gaze to the hostages briefly, the fear in their eyes overwhelming. Deep down, Vincent knew they were more afraid of him than they were of the gangs.

He closed his eyes and swallowed the desire to skim Badou down the street like a stone across a pond. Now appearing docile enough, the group escorted Vincent from the street. This would not go unpunished. They would pay for making a fool out of him.

"LET'S GO!" Badou yelled.

Gang members began to spill out of the surrounding houses, following closely behind.

***

The sound of metal connecting with bone echoed throughout an abandoned warehouse in the old industrial district. The heavy noise bouncing off the thin metal walls and high ceilings, was almost drowned out by the laughter of the large, unruly group of gangsters.

Cold chains were secured tightly around Vincent's wrists and ankles, restricting his movements, and suspending him from the support beams in the rusted metal ceiling. His feet were bound and bolted to the heavily stained, concrete floor.

The faint smell of the dried blood from previous hostages caused him more anguish than his confinement.

Holding a damaged, metal bat, one man swung ruthlessly at Vincent's skull and chest. Yet, despite his best efforts, it only bent the weapon further.

"That's it, my turn!" another demanded. "So, you're saying that if I stick this piece of shit with a blade, it won't do a thing?"

He looked at Badou for confirmation.

"Knock yourself out," Badou replied wearily. "The Vipers have had more run-ins with this freak than all the other gangs combined. So, we understand not many of you have had the chance to put his body to the test."

The man stepped forward, thrusting the knife into Vincent's abdomen. He began to tremble as he applied more and more pressure. However, to the man's disappointment, he was forced to withdraw—the knife having no more effect than a finger pressing against skin.

He tried again—this time, applying all his strength, but the blade snapped off at the handle. Breathing heavily from his wasted effort, the man looked furiously up at Vincent.

"You done already?" Vincent asked with a self-righteous look on his face. He was used to this. The Vipers had tried to hurt him many times before, and this time was no different. Their weapons had no effect. He could barely feel anything but a light itch.

The man reached for another weapon.

"That's enough!" Badou shoved the man aside. "Any more is just a waste of time and good weapons."

"You wanna tell me why I'm here?" Vincent yawned. "Earlier, you said you'd put me in the dirt once and for all. How exactly are you gonna do that?"

"I was waiting for that cocky attitude to come out before the main show," Badou smiled. "You think just because you're super strong that your body is invincible?"

"You haven't drawn a single drop of blood yet. Who knows? Maybe you'll bore me to death."

Badou walked into the crowd and was handed an object wrapped in cloth. He unveiled a handgun and pointed it at Vincent's head.

"W-where did, where did you get a gun?!" He hadn't known Badou to be a murderer, but Vincent was horrified that he had managed to get his hands on a firearm. This was dangerous, not for him but for everyone who lived in the ghetto.

"She's a beauty, ain't she?" Badou stroked the barrel of the gun, drinking in Vincent's horror. "And that's not even the best part."

He stretched his arms out, and several gang members pulled back a cloth at the back of the warehouse, revealing a massive pile of firearms of all shapes and sizes.

"Turns out, our new unified group is capable of some pretty amazing things."

Badou threw his head back and laughed maniacally. "By sharing our information and resources, we've been able to acquire these through the underbelly of the Metropolis. We now have a deal to supply firearms in the ghettos!"

However, Vincent had stopped listening.

Badou's words had faded out as he stared at the gun pointed at his face. His mind wandered back to when he was a child.

***

Venturing into the Ryuuga Metropolis under the cover of darkness, a young Vincent ran playfully alongside two other children. A boy around his age, and a young girl slightly older. The girl's long, fiery-red hair billowed behind her as she ran. She laughed playfully, looking back at Vincent with her emerald eyes. Vincent blushed, admiring her beauty. The boy had spikey, short, light grey hair and a surprisingly muscular physique for a child his age.

They ran about the large city without a care in the world—regardless of what the Metropolitan residents thought of them. The mischievous trio hid in dark alleys before sprinting into local convenience stores and stealing all their little arms could carry.

One night, Vincent was on lookout duty while the

other young boy ran from an incapacitated resident with a fistful of cash. Suddenly, a police officer sprang into action, catching the boy and beating him ruthlessly before pulling out a gun. He cocked back the hammer and hesitated for what felt like an eternity.

***

BANG!

Badou had fired a warning shot into the air—the sound reverberated through the desolate shed. "Wakey Wakey!" he crowed with a wicked grin. "I'm sorry. Do you have somewhere else to be? Doesn't matter because you can dream all you want in just a second."

Badou held the barrel up to Vincent's forehead as he began to tremble.

What is this sensation? This feeling? He wondered.

Doubt, confusion, anger, despair. They were all flooding through his mind. He was paralyzed, and not because of the chains restricting him. It was the sudden onslaught of raw, unbridled emotion surging throughout his body.

Is this fear? Vincent thought, as the barrel of the

handgun slid across his forehead and pressed into his temple.

"Sweet dreams, Mr. Hero," Badou exclaimed as he pulled the trigger.

<u>Chapter Two</u>

Vincent slowly opened his eyes. A dizzying sensation, mixed with high-pitched ringing, drowned out the sound of muffled voices.

The compact remains of a bullet rocked back and forth on the ground beneath his feet. Vincent shook his head; his balance and hearing were slightly impaired, but the effects were quick to wear off.

He was alive and no worse off than before.

"I-I-that's Impossible." Badou dropped his handgun

in disbelief. "HOW ARE YOU STILL ALIVE?!?" he roared.

"Well, that was unexpected."

Vincent raised his head, staring at the rusted metal ceiling. "For a moment there, I think I was actually afraid to die. It's been a long time since I felt scared like that."

He let out a bark of laughter, meeting Badou's eyes.

"Thanks for that!" Vincent acknowledged, grinning gleefully.

Badou stepped backward as the chains holding Vincent's arms suddenly tightened, snapping free from the beams above. He threw off the remaining shackles from around his feet and stretched out.

Badou and his gang stood by, amazed at what they had just witnessed. A man was shot in the head without so much as a scratch, and now, he was ready to attack.

They raised their weapons, arms shaking with fear. One, braver than the rest, leapt forward and slammed a pipe against the back of Vincent's head. Vincent rocked forward and was caught off balance. Suddenly, he spun around, imbedding his fist into the man's face, and hurtling him into a far-off corner of the warehouse—the fight was on.

Vincent was a whirlwind of punches, kicks, and headbutts—throwing bodies far and wide as Badou skulked away in the confusion. Oblivious to this fact; Vincent was positively joyous as he tore through the sea of violent thugs who had attempted to stab, shoot, and murder him mere moments earlier.

This was it, the battle he was looking for when he was awoken from his slumber in the alley.

Badou picked up his sword and an arm full of guns and as the massacre continued, he stumbled down the narrow alley between the warehouses. Suddenly, Vincent's leg penetrated the warehouse wall.

"Wakey Wakey!" Vincent sneered from the other side.

His fingers burst through the wall, and he peeled the metal open with ease.

"I'm sorry, do you have somewhere else to be? Well, doesn't matter because you can dream all you want in just a second!" he said, parroting Badou's mockery from earlier.

***

As the sun began to set, a bright orange hue lit the rusted and worn remains of the warehouse district. Shadows slowly crept over a horde of unconscious bodies strewn throughout the warehouse with a mangled pile of firearms at its center.

Vincent soared through the sky, jumping from building to building, carrying Badou's unconscious body. He soon arrived at the base of an impossibly high cliff and began leaping upwards, bouncing on several natural ledges up to the top.

Vincent dropped Badou chest-first onto the soil, his head hanging over the edge, and waited for him to regain consciousness. He stirred, and Vincent quickly put a foot on Badou's back, pinning his chest to the ground. Badou snapped awake in a panic struggling with all his might.

"Aint it funny how our roles are suddenly reversed?" Vincent questioned as he hopped off Badou's back. Grabbing the thug by one ankle, he yanked Badou upwards, holding him upside down over the deadly drop.

Rather than looking down upon the ghetto as he expected, Badou saw a vast, vacant field. This surprise was quickly replaced with terror again, as he struggled against Vincent's vice-like grip.

The sun had set now, and the sky was a beautiful twilight blue.

"Did you know that I come up here and eat every afternoon at sunset?" Vincent asked.

"And do you know what I think about while I'm here?"

Badou continued to flail nervously but kept quiet.

"I think about leaving," Vincent continued, staring off into the distance.

"You think you're slick because you got your hands on some guns? You know the rules, man. We bring in anything we can from the Metropolis. Food, drink gadgets…shit, even the garbage that the 'cloud people' throw away. Anything and everything is traded in the ghettos. But not guns, never guns."

Vincent paused; a disappointed grimace crept across

his face.

"It won't be long until the Metro police find out that you brought them in here. They'll tear this place apart, looking for hidden weapons and other illegal goods. All because of you."

Badou scoffed as Vincent pressed on.

"The cloud people already think less of us because of the stigmata," he explained, caressing a mysterious marking that stained the skin around his throat.

"Nobody knows why we all have these marks, where they come from, or even what they do, if anything. All we know is that everyone in the ghettos is born with one, and they're the reason we were caged like animals for centuries. Even now with the gates open, we aren't given proper jobs or housing, or other basic rights outside the ghetto. Shit, we aren't even treated like people! They call us dogs because it looks like we have collars around our necks. And so, we're looked down on like animals, feeding off their leftovers. The city barely lets our people work the shitty jobs they don't want to do themselves. Those bastards might ban us from working in the

Metropolis if you give em enough reason. You and I mightn't have jobs, man, but plenty of people down there live on the money they bring in from that place!"

Vincent pulled Badou's quivering body closer and shook him violently.

"I'm not gonna let you screw all that up for them!" He snarled, extending his arm again as if to drop Badou head-first over the cliff's edge.

A wet patch formed in the crotch of Badou's pants and dribbled across his stomach.

"You pissed yourself!" Vincent cackled. "The mighty Badou actually pissed his pants!"

Thoroughly entertained, Vincent flung Badou backward into the dirt, holding his stomach as he bent over with laughter.

"W-W-What are you going to do with me?" Badou uttered nervously, still focused on his whereabouts atop a giant cliff face.

"Are you going to kill me up here?"

Vincent wiped away the tears from his eyes.

"No, but I probably should. Nothing I do ever seems

to stop you," he sighed.

"The ghetto has it bad enough without you and those other pieces of shit running around, making it worse for everyone."

Vincent couldn't hide the sadness in his voice.

"Ya' know, I was gonna tie you up naked in the middle of town and let all the people you terrorized have their revenge. Who knows, maybe that would teach you some humility. But…it would probably still end up the same way as it always does. You'd go back to committing crimes, and I'd go back to stopping you." The pattern had remained the same for so many years.

"I don't understand why you keep hurtin' these people, and you don't understand why I keep saving em. Meanwhile, there's a whole town down there, caught in the middle of it all, just struggling to get by and make ends meet."

"Why?" Badou asked curiously. "Why do you bother? No one wants *your* help."

Vincent ignored him.

"But, as I was draggin' your ass back into town, "I

looked up at the cliffs and got to thinking, maybe you've never seen things my way because you've never seen the ghetto the way only I can. I'm the only one who can get up here, so perhaps it might help you to see for yourself."

Badou hesitated and got to his feet, moving to stand a few paces behind Vincent.

"Why does it look like that?" he asked with genuine curiosity.

"What do you see down there?" Vincent pointed out over the false green scenery beneath them.

Badou was usually quick to react; however, words had escaped him this time. He knew he was high above the ghettos, yet what he faced was impossibly beautiful greenery and rolling fields he had never seen in his life. He paused for a moment.

"We all know the wall around the ghetto, right? Vincent said, waiting for Badou's hesitant nod. "And until a few hundred years ago, the gates were sealed shut—cornering us between the cliffs and the Metropolis itself. Well, …this is what our home looks like from the other side. Whether it was back before the gates opened up or sometime after, a fancy barrier was put in place to make our home look more appealing.

Badou clenched his teeth in frustration. "I had no idea!"

Vincent tilted his head back, staring into the clouds.

"C'mon, man, you know how it is here; the metropolis is for the rich, and the ghetto is for the poor. The Ryuuga Metropolis: The city of opportunity. Can you believe that?" Vincent scoffed. "We see them, sitting in their precious high-rise buildings, and we think they're looking down on us, right? When it's far worse. I guess nobody wants to live in the sky and see our filthy homes down below."

"And you're okay with that?" Badou snapped back.

Vincent shrugged.

"Don't ignore me, Vincent. I'm asking if that shit bothers you."

Vincent had been looking far off into the distance, yet he could feel Badou's unflinching gaze. Fear and hatred seem to go hand in hand most of the time. But Badou had never really feared Vincent, though he did appear to share the ghetto's hatred of him.

"Of course, it bothers me." Vincent snapped.

"But that city could probably wipe out the ghetto entirely if it wanted to. Then where would we go? The nearest village is weeks away on foot, and nobody would have enough rations to make the trip. Even the supplies you and your goons stole would probably only get a handful of families outta here. And then what? Who's to say it's any safer out in the unknown? Honestly, we're lucky that those bastards are content with just hiding us behind a barrier."

"What the hell is that supposed to mean?" Badou snarled.

"Lucky...LUCKY?! You're sayin' that we should be thankful for those rich assholes?

Vincent remained unusually calm, despite Badou's sudden outburst.

"That's not what I'm saying. But it's not like anyone can change things."

"You could," Badou replied.

Vincent was stunned—finally, Badou had

acknowledged him. He realized that this was also the most that they had ever spoken. The irony was not lost on Vincent. He yearned for Badou's friendship and acceptance when he was younger. But as time passed, Badou's rebellious and violent tendencies only further divided them—and eventually, they became foes.

The residents of the ghetto were either cruel or terrified of him. Children always liked Vincent, but they seemed to think of him as a sideshow attraction rather than a person.

Vincent turned his gaze back over to the large city of ornate gold and bronze—its buildings reaching high into the clouds.

"Maybe I could change things. I mean, it's not like I haven't thought about it."

Vincent had, in fact, contemplated this idea many times.

"Then why don't you?" Badou asked sharply.

"You have super strength; your body is practically invincible, and you can jump all the way up here! You could probably take over that entire city if you wanted to!"

Vincent laughed at Badou's flattery.

"Look, I know I'm the only one living in the ghettos with this power. But I don't think I'm the only one out there. I think there may be others like me."

Badou looked up at Vincent, eyeing him skeptically.

"There used to be two other kids with strength like mine." Vincent winced a little inside. He didn't like to remember them, but he felt that explaining this to Badou was necessary. Badou never knew them or noticed the three young mischievous children that ran in the shadows of the ghetto when Vincent was young.

"What happened to them?" Badou asked, his curiosity quelling his anger.

Vincent's head dropped a little, and the shadows of his hat covered his eyes.

"One of em died." He said flatly.

"Shot in the head by a Metro cop."

Badou's face fell.

"I'm…I'm sorry."

Ignoring Badou's apology, though it sounded

genuine, Vincent continued.

"It's not like we were entirely innocent. The three of us were stealin' food from the convenience stores in the Metro after hours. Selina was kinda strong." Vincent smiled sadly, remembering her wild and fierce nature.

"I mean, she was stronger than most adults, even when she was eleven. But Ren and I were different. We were both only seven, and we were way stronger. It was like night n day." Vincent reminisced, grinning slightly for a moment before his expression fell again.

"But one day, Ren went too far and started beating up people for cash. Selina refused to be a part of it, and Ren used to make me be the lookout."

Vincent hesitated. This was personal. Too personal. He'd got a little carried away and found himself speaking too freely. He shook his head to reset his thoughts and carefully considered his next words.

"Then what?" Badou asked impatiently.

"Ren got caught." Vincent slowly continued as if omitting something from the story.

"He was beaten…badly by a cop who seemed to have

strength like ours. That's when he pulled out his gun and shot Ren in the head, point-blank. Just like you did to me."

"Look, man, I had no idea…"

Vincent raised his hand, interrupting Badou's attempt to apologize, and changed the subject.

"Who knows. Maybe I could do something. But ya know what stops me from leaving every single time I come up here?" Vincent looked up and smiled thinly.

"Knowing the people down there aren't safe while people like you are wandering about."

Vincent's expression grew cold.

"You weren't always like this, Badou. I mean, you always had a bad attitude, but you never really hurt people. Then you just snapped and created the Vipers to terrorize everyone."

Badou's face fell and what little color he had left fled his face.

"I mean, you guys did start doing a little better as a result," Vincent sighed.

"But that's around the same time I started beatin' your

asses…so it's hard to say if it was worth it or not."

"Yeah, you're right; I never used to be like this," Badou replied harshly.

"Then, one day, I got sick of being a victim, so I started taking what I wanted instead of beggin' for it like a loser! Everyone down there is nothing more than a victim, and I refuse to be one of em."

"But that's not *their* fault," Vincent scolded. "We're all victims of circumstance…and attacking us won't make any real change."

"THEN WHAT ARE WE SUPPOSED TO DO?!" Badou shouted, tears beginning to prick the corners of his eyes.

He had felt the same for so long. But now, Vincent could see the big lug was finally showing a softer side.

"Not sure," Vincent said quietly.

"Like I said, maybe I can make a difference. Maybe I can leave this place and get help…find out what's through that forest and find a new place for us all."

Vincent pointed his thumb backward toward a dense thicket of green bushland behind them.

"If that's true, why haven't you done anything yet?" Badou scoffed.

"What? And leave this place unprotected? Who in the hell do you think will keep an eye on the ghettos to make sure people like you don't take advantage?!" Vincent sneered, baring his teeth.

Badou turned away and looked down the jagged cliff face.

"As I said, they don't want your help—they never did. Besides, what do you want me to do about it?" he asked petulantly.

Despite being several years older, Badou suddenly looked ashamed. Being lectured as if he were a child only added to his humiliation.

Vincent reached out to place a hand on his shoulder—shoving Badou slightly.

"It'd be nice if I could count on you to protect these people instead of making things worse. They have it hard enough, and you're strong." Vincent grinned mischievously.

"Granted, not as strong as me, but they need someone

who can help them if I'm not around. It's like you said…they don't want *my* help."

"Do you think you could actually change things from the outside?" Badou turned to face Vincent. All his swagger and petulant aggression were gone. Behind it, Vincent knew Badou could be a man that everyone in the ghetto could look up to—just as he once did when he was younger.

"Not sure. But we won't know until I try. I'm not even sure how long I'd be away. Besides, how can I trust you after all you've done? How do I know you won't go down there and destroy everything the second you know I'm gone?" Vincent eyed Badou suspiciously.

"I guess…you don't. But seeing this makes me understand our home is just a joke to the Metropolis."

"Out of sight, out of mind, right?" Vincent added.

"Nothing's gonna change if we don't do things differently," Badou agreed, his voice quivering. "They say we will be given a fair shot, but that's bullshit. Those people just see the stigmata and laugh at us. They ignore us, and even beat us. We feed off their scraps, and now this. This view just proves how little they think of us!"

"Yeah, I get that," Vincent replied. "Why do you think I brought you up here? Do you really think a few people with guns would change that much? They already think of us as animals. Sure; you might have wanted to rebel against that place, but do you really think acting like a monster is proving them wrong?"

Vincent's words cut Badou. Deep down, he knew he was right.

Vincent stretched his arms towards the night sky, interlacing his fingers.

"Besides, I scrunched up all those guns like big balls of paper." he smiled broadly—proud of his handiwork.

Badou laughed heartily and smiled at Vincent.

"You really are a freak. Ya know that? I mean, who doesn't die from a gunshot to the head at point-blank range?"

Vincent smiled for a split second before his memory of Ren quickly took him back.

The visibility of the stars began to dim slightly as the Metropolis came alive with a dazzling display of artificial light.

"So, where do we go from here?" Badou asked. "You can't trust me, and you said you wouldn't kill me."

"Not sure," Vincent replied, exasperated. Could he really leave this place? The possibilities and the risks were endless and only added to his anxiety.

"It's not like I can run off and get help tomorrow. But I can't just sit around and do nothing either."

Badou reached out and punched Vincent in the shoulder lightly.

"I'll talk to the boys, and we'll see if I can keep them from causing any more trouble."

Vincent was relieved to hear this finally.

"You'd better, or everyone's gonna know the mighty Badou, head of the Vipers and the most freighting delinquent of the ghetto, peed himself."

A red flush crept up Badou's neck to his face.

"HEY!" He shouted, covering his pants with his hands.

"Don't worry, you behave, and nobody has ta know," Vincent reassured. Badou would never live this down, and Vincent would never let him forget it.

He gave Badou a wicked grin, "Let's get outta here."

"Wait a sec." Badou interrupted. "Those two friends of yours…"

Vincent stopped smiling instantly—twisting his head to avoid eye contact.

"Yeah, what of em?"

Badou fidgeted a little, struggling to voice the words he wanted to say.

"I-I mean…if you survived a gunshot to the head, maybe your friend did too!"

Vincent looked down at the dirt.

"Yeah, after your little attempt to murder me earlier, I started wonderin' bout that too. But he did die that day. I was there. Maybe it was the beating the officer gave him beforehand. Or maybe it's because we were young, so our bodies hadn't developed enough or something, I dunno."

"What about your other friend…the girl. What happened to her?"

Vincent looked hard at Badou.

"Not sure. After Ren died, she left me and the ghetto behind." The finality in his voice stopped Badou from prying any further.

Badou turned his back to Vincent, furiously rubbing the tears that had begun to sting his eyes.

Careful not to let this mushy moment continue, Vincent quickly grabbed Badou by the back of the jacket and leapt off the cliff. With his petrified screams echoing throughout the ghetto district below, Badou's body flapped helplessly in the wind—bringing a faint smile to Vincent's face.

Maybe things really could change.

Chapter Three

After dropping Badou home, Vincent made his way along the moonlit streets to the old industrial district. He was planning to dispose of what remained of the guns and check in on the unconscious gang members that he had littered across the area earlier.

As he walked, he smiled to himself, feeling a deep sense of satisfaction and wondering if things might finally be a little different.

Vincent was so lost in thought that he barely noticed

a figure hidden in the shadows, leaning against a metal roller door to one of the warehouses.

Just as Vincent passed by, the man spoke.

"Well, *you* certainly had a productive day," The man remained in the shadows, just out of sight.

Vincent lunged backward instinctively. Life in the ghetto had taught him to always be on guard and ready for a fight. It wasn't every day someone could take him by surprise.

"Who are you?" Vincent growled aggressively.

He knew everyone who lived in the ghetto, either by face or name, yet he didn't recognize the man standing before him.

"If you're looking for the guns and those guys you dealt with earlier. I took care of them while you were up on the cliffs with that Badou guy."

The stranger sauntered out of the shadows. He wore long brown pants, a grey and white hoodie, and an eyepatch with a metal crucifix design that caught the moonlight.

Vincent withdrew a few steps—the hairs on the back

of his neck stood on end. Every cell in his body urged him to retreat. But Vincent had never run from a fight in his life, and despite the stranger's ominous presence, he wasn't about to start now.

"Whaddya mean you *took care of them*?" Vincent didn't like the gangs, but he didn't want them killed. The man smirked and stepped further into the moonlight.

"Both the guns *and* the gang members are with the authorities of Ryuuga Metro. But can you trust Badou? Sounds like you two have history. I can have him arrested and taken out of here too, if it makes things easier."

The man unfolded his arms and placed them in the pockets of his hoodie.

"Had them arrested? WHO SAID YOU COULD DO THAT?!" Vincent shouted. Suddenly, he stopped, noticing that the man didn't bear the stigmata around his throat. Vincent took a moment to compose himself. This must be an officer from the Metropolis. He recoiled slightly.

"Look, I know we aren't supposed to have guns in

here, but I dealt with it. You saw them, right? I destroyed them all."

Vincent paused, his eyes narrowing.

"Wait. If you were here, arresting those guys, how did you know what Badou and I were talking about up on the cliffs?"

"Your mind's quite sharp. That's good. Looks like you might have some potential, after all, Vincent."

Vincent's eyes widened. How in the hell did this guy know his name? It's not that people in the ghetto didn't know him. They all did. But this was a stranger. Heat flooded his cheeks as he tried to remain calm.

The man smiled at Vincent and took a few steps toward him. "Those men were trash; they fed upon the weak and hurt innocent people. They weren't going to just fall in line, even *if* Badou told them to. Trust me. They're better off in jail."

"You didn't answer my question," Vincent interrupted. "How did you know what I was talking about with Badou on the cliffs if you were down here?"

An entertained grin lit the man's face.

"Check the top of your hat."

Vincent took off his cap and inspected it, finding nothing out of the ordinary. The stranger took his hands out of his pockets, pulling back his right sleeve and tapping a button on a small strap around his wrist. A shimmer of blue light appeared on Vincent's hat, revealing a tiny metal device no bigger than a match head.

"What's this thing?" Vincent stared at the device. He had never seen anything like it before.

"That's a transceiver. A tiny bug that allows us to track a person's whereabouts and listen to their conversations."

"This…this thing…*you* put it on me?" Vincent's anger bubbled to the surface. "When?" he asked sharply.

"Oh, that's been on you for about seven days now. I was surprised by how easy it was to get close to a guy who prides himself on how *guarded* and *tough* he is…Mr. Hero."

He gestured with air quotes to Vincent's fury.

"You've been watching *and* listening to me for seven

days?" Vincent felt a vein in his temple throb.

"That's right. Would you like to know why?"

Vincent looked up, meeting the man's belittling gaze. "Haven't you people taken enough from us?"

Mistreatment from the residents of the Metropollis was not unusual, but he couldn't stop the deep sadness that still filled his heart. "Does even our privacy belong to the sky people now too?"

The stranger reared his head back and smiled. His smirk shocked Vincent to the core. How could he find this amusing?

"I never said that I was from the Ryuuga Metro," the man stated suspiciously.

Vincent was lost for words—struggling to comprehend what the man had insinuated.

"I...don't understand, I thought—"

"You *thought* wrong because of your ignorance. The world is a big place, Vincent, and there are more people out there than the ones living here."

Vincent took a step forward without even realizing it.

"Then why did you arrest everyone? Just who are

you? Where are you from? I-I-I don't understand."

"Who I am isn't important right now, and I come from a place that I doubt you've heard of. The reason we have been observing you is because of your power. It's not often we see a Melee Meister of your caliber without specialist training."

We? Melee Meister? Vincent's head was spinning. He needed answers, but every time the man spoke, it just raised more questions.

Careful not to distract himself further, Vincent tried to stay on topic. "And the others? Why arrest them if you aren't even *from* here? Did you think you were doing the right thing or something?"

Vincent softened his posture, as he began to explain the situation further.

"Look, here in the ghettos, we handle things ourselves…without getting the Metro involved. Those bastards don't exactly have our best interests at heart."

"Yeah, I've noticed that. There's definitely a strained relationship between the people of the ghetto and citizens of Ryuuga."

"WE...ARE RYUUGA!" Vincent corrected aggressively. "We were here first. That...*city* came along long after."

"Woah, calm down, slugger. I wasn't trying to offend. I was just—"

The man hesitated for a moment. Finally, his face shifted to reveal a devious lopsided grin.

"Truth is, I was doing you a favor."

"What's that supposed ta mean?" Vincent felt uneasy about where this conversation was heading. He didn't know this stranger, but it was clear that he wanted something from Vincent.

"In the time I spent watching you, all you did was laze around all day and fight. You'd wake up and go looking for trouble or wait until trouble found you. Then, you'd jump up that cliff at the end of every damned day and think about leaving. But the truth is, you were never going to leave. Not while you had to worry about those guys." The man chuckled lightly.

"Hell, you said as much while you were up there spilling your heart to Badou earlier. I don't just *think* I did the right thing. I *know I* did the right thing."

Vincent's chest tightened as he struggled valiantly to control the deep-rooted rage inside him. This outsider didn't know the first thing about his struggles. Yet, there was a kernel of truth to his accusation. Vincent shook his head.

"Listen, you can't just—"

"No, you listen. You get off on helping people. You're the big fish in a small pond, and it's just the way you like it. It's quite pathetic, really. Besides, from what I can tell, everyone here is terrified of you. Probably because none of them seem to know what a Meister is here. But that's beside the point." The man shook his head. "Regardless, you just recycle those thugs, using them as punching bags while you play the hero over and over again. You wanted a reason to leave; well, now you have one...No need to thank me."

Vincent grabbed the tiny transceiver and crushed it between his fingers.

"Let me get this straight, you don't live here...or even in the Metropolis for that matter! But you come in, unannounced and uninvited, and spy on me?"

Vincent's muscles tightened as his body thrummed in anger.

"And you dare call *me* arrogant? Look, I'm strong enough to take care of myself…I don't need some *kid* calling the shots and deciding what's best for everyone."

The mysterious man stiffened slightly, and his eye twitched. He was shorter than Vincent but only by a few inches.

Content with the moral victory, Vincent turned to walk away. It wasn't worthwhile to fight someone from outside the walls and potentially cause more trouble for the residents.

"Petulant child." He replied smugly. "You don't know the first thing about what it means to be strong".

Vincent stopped in his tracks with his shoulders hunched. He turned back slowly, biting his lower lip while the corner of his mouth twitched to a sneer.

"Are you *trying* to start a fight?"

The stranger sauntered over until he was nearly nose-to-nose with Vincent.

"I'm not *trying*, and it wouldn't be much of a fight." Vincent cracked his neck from side to side and took a fighting stance.

The intruder pulled his sleeve back down and put his hands back into the pockets of his hoodie—an evil now present on his face.

"I guess we're doing this then," Vincent stated calmly. "I hope you're ready for this."

"There's that arrogance again," the young man replied. "Let's just see what Ryuuga's Hero is made of, shall we?"

***

Although sporting a vast amount of open space, the industrial district was mostly avoided by the residents of the ghetto.

This was Viper territory.

Graffiti marked the floors, doors, and walls, and several metal bins littered the district— used as firepits during the night.

While the area was usually filled with rambunctious delinquents, the maze of concrete and metal was now filled with an eerie silence.

Strong winds blew between the narrow alleyways that barely separated some of the buildings, emitting a howling sound that added to the haunted ambiance of the moonlit industrial graveyard.

Suddenly, the sound of destruction thundered across the vacant labyrinth of metal constructs.

Buildings collapsed, pillars were thrown clear from their foundations, and large portions of the ground were blown open as Vincent and the stranger fought with the force of a natural disaster.

Several cracks spread through the old factory's thick, concrete wall, before crumbling—leaving a gaping hole where Vincent had fallen through.

Gasping for air, Vincent wiped the dirt and dust from his face with the back of his hand. He looked down, perplexed at the dark red smear across his skin and the strange metallic taste in his mouth.

He couldn't remember the last time he had ever experienced pain, much less had blood drawn in a fight.

What is this feeling? Vincent thought, a maniacal grin

spreading across his face. His heart was racing, and he could feel the blood coursing through his veins. He wasn't scared; he wasn't even tempted to run. Instead, he was exhilarated.

"Who in the hell are you?" he whispered.

"I'm the guy teaching you a lesson," the man confidently replied, his clothes still immaculate with not a hair out of place.

Vincent slowly rose to his feet.

"Your attitude really pisses me off. But to be honest, I can't remember the last time I've had this much fun in a fight. Nobody's ever made me work *this* hard," Vincent replied eagerly. Bouncing on the balls of his feet, he took up a boxing stance.

"If you're having fun, that means I'm not doing my job." the man said coldly, adjusting the glove on his left hand and pulling it tight.

Vincent made the first move, darting forwards with enough explosive power to create a small crater where he had been standing. He swung wildly, missing by a hair's breadth, as the man casually evaded each strike.

Vincent continued with a flurry of punches and kicks until the man unexpectedly caught hold of the back of Vincent's head, slamming his face into a thrusted knee.

Vincent momentarily lost consciousness as his head bounced upward with a stream of blood spewing from his nose.

He threw Vincent back to the ground before delivering a lightning-fast kick to his solar plexus.

Vincent held his sides, struggling to breathe. He was clearly outmatched.

Blood trickled from his mouth and down his chin. He looked up, only to see his opponent standing over him with a cold, murderous intent.

"Still having fun?" the man asked, unimpressed with Vincent's lack of ability.

Vincent clambered onto his hands and knees. His vision was blurred, and his body ached—nevertheless, he smiled maniacally. Adrenaline rushed through Vincent's body, and it felt like every cell was on fire.

Vincent laughed under his breath, but before he could utter a word in response, the man's foot struck Vincent firmly in the teeth.

On the other side of the compound, a heavy, thick wall crushed inward, with Vincent embedded among the debris

With Vincent momentarily incapacitated, the man walked casually across the lot. His menacing shadow stretched out across the warehouse floor as he entered.

Careful not to show his pain, Vincent spat blood from his mouth and rubbed his tongue across the backs of his teeth. Miraculously, they were still in place.

Their eyes met, and the color drained from Vincent's face. He didn't know how much longer he would be able to keep this up. So far, he hadn't managed to land a single blow. His vision was dark around the edges, and his thoughts slowed.

"You're strong, but I expected a lot more. Listen, you might be able to beat some street thugs like it's nothing…but in my world, you're weak!" Every word he spoke dripped with contempt. "You have raw talent, but you don't know how to use it. Come find me when you want to know what *true* strength is."

He turned to walk away, but as he did so, Vincent's silhouette rose from the ground—a red glow emanating from his body.

The stranger stopped and smiled expectantly. "Well then, are we finally ready to take this seriously?"

He turned around slowly and marveled at the sight before him.

A series of markings had stretched across Vincent's face, arms, legs, and chest. They glowed a bright red, with yellow portions of energy surging throughout.

"Interesting," the man took a half step back.

"Looks like you—"

Without warning, a powerful punch slammed into his face.

The sheer sound of the impact shook the ground beneath their feet, and the man was sent hurtling out into the open district—crashing into a building across the far side of the lot.

Vincent suddenly felt a sharp surge of pain travel through his arm. It radiated from the tips of his fingers right through to his shoulder, hurting him tremendously.

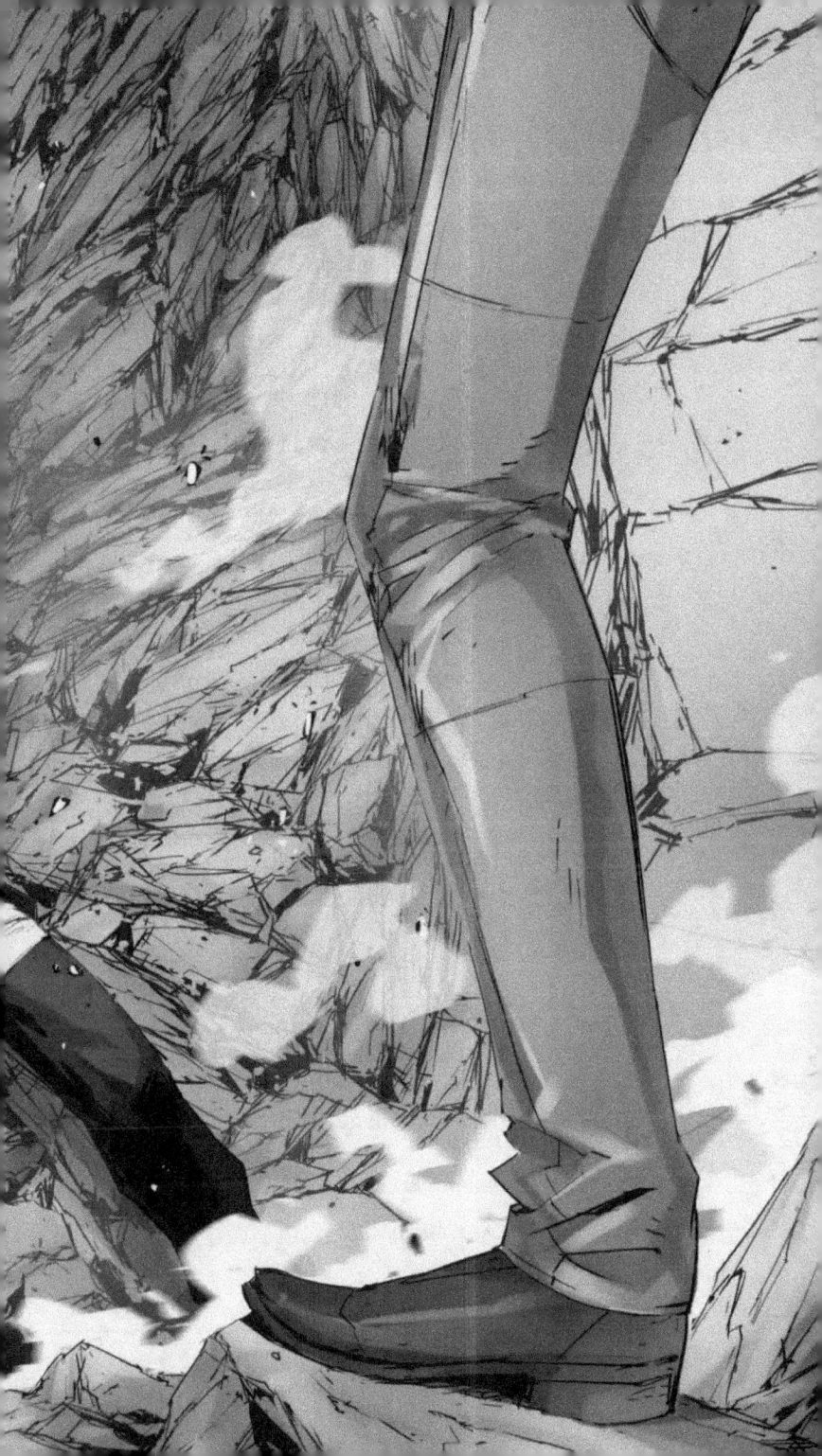

Still, this was the power he needed to win. He shook out his arms— trying to wave away the discomfort.

Bursting up through the broken concrete debris, the man emerged, slightly shaken from the impact.

"Okay," he said, taking a deep breath. "So, you're a little—."

A clap of thunder erupted as Vincent closed the distance between them, launching another attack.

The noise and vibrations from this strike rattled the foundations of the district itself. Only this time, the stranger hadn't moved. Blocking Vincent's blow, the stranger held two huge handguns; one crossed over the other.

The large guns resembled Desert Eagle semi-automatic pistols. Although they were identical in shape and design, their color differed; one was ivory, the other onyx.

Both pistols glistened beautifully in the moonlight, drawing attention to the golden cross that ran from muzzle to hammer on both sides.

"Sorry, not this time," he grunted.

Vincent chuckled, ignoring the second wave of pain as his fist pressed against the weapons.

"What happened to getting rid of the guns, huh?" Vincent asked.

His opponent's expression turned icy-cold, murderous intent filling the air again.

"Don't mistake *these* for those pieces of scrap!" he growled, pushing harder against Vincent before flicking his arms outward. Vincent flew back a few meters, his feet scraping across the ground.

As he came to a stop, Vincent noticed that the pistols had vanished. There were no visible holsters or pouches on the man, apart from the pockets of his hoodie, which couldn't possibly hold weapons of that size.

"Where'd your little pea-shooters go?"

"I wonder," the man replied calmly, ignoring Vincent's attempt to goad him.

Vincent darted in swiftly, only this time; he received an extremely heavy punch to the face.

His head rocked back from the impact. But before he could recover, he was inundated with a series of hooks, jabs, and uppercuts.

Even though these attacks still hurt, they felt different from the initial blow.

They felt…lighter, and they lacked weight. Regardless, Vincent still struggled to regain his composure and end the tirade.

Panic threatened to overwhelm him. His breathing hitched as he tucked his chin down to his chest, raising his hands and shielding his head from the barrage of punches.

His right arm still felt oddly weak from the pain that had set in, and he noticed that the red markings were beginning to fade.

It was a night of firsts for Vincent. He had never in his life felt this weak. But his resolution to persevere did not waiver. His single-minded determination and willpower held strong.

In response to Vincent's tight guard, the attacker quickly shifted his feet, bobbing and twisting his upper body, before throwing a powerful uppercut. It slipped between Vincent's elbows and struck him in the jaw—

rattling his brain.

Vincent's head rocked upwards, and his hat was sent flying. The red markings covering his body flickered, and his arms fell lifelessly by his side.

Careful not to give Vincent a moment's rest, the man grabbed the front of his singlet and delivered a final, thunderous strike into his stomach.

Vincent doubled over as the air suddenly abandoned his lungs.

"That all you got?" Vincent coughed out breathlessly, hunched over with blood running down his chin and hair strewn across his face.

The man threw a downward punch to land the deciding blow. Only this time, Vincent stopped it, catching the man by the wrist.

"Y-You haven't won yet." Vincent stuttered with an air of self-assured confidence.

The man stared back at Vincent with an emotionless expression.

"Is that right?"

Suddenly, a massive blast of white and blue light

appeared from the man's hand. It exploded directly into Vincent's face—sending him tumbling backward and violently skipping across the concrete.

Vincent slammed his hand into the ground, bracing his legs and sliding to a stop.

What the hell was that? He'd never seen such an attack before.

He looked up, smoke sizzling from his face. But the man had vanished.

Vincent looked around, frantically searching… but he saw nothing but empty space and the destruction their fight had caused.

"COWARD!" he yelled aggressively as his breath returned to him.

Vincent waited a few more seconds in anticipation, but there was nothing. Not a sound nor flash of movement anywhere. On edge and grinding his teeth, Vincent let out a breath he didn't know he had been holding. He turned to walk away, holding his injured right arm. But as he did so, he came face to face with the man—both arms extended to Vincent's chest. Another strange light flashed and erupted from his palms, blasting Vincent backward again.

Somehow, he managed to remain on his feet. *What the hell was going on here?* He had never seen anyone move without so much as a sound. And what was with these lights?

Vincent's heart raced. He wasn't used to struggling in a fight, and his ego felt as bruised as his body.

Then he noticed something odd. Although the attack had enough force to push him back, it hadn't done any damage.

He's run out of power! Vincent thought to himself excitedly.

Dashing in at full speed, he hoped to catch his opponent off-guard, only to receive a perfectly timed and heavy blow to the face.

The man had anticipated Vincent's attack and countered it with precise accuracy.

Then, the world changed.

Everything was suddenly covered in a green hue, distorting the landscape and taking everything out of focus.

Darkness faded in and out of sight while everything began to duplicate and spin.

At that moment, Vincent found himself unable to comprehend the dazzling display of color and twisted scenery.

***

Vincent's eyes shot open.

Did...did I fall asleep? he wondered groggily. He was flat on his back, staring up at the night sky. Everything ached.

The man suddenly appeared in his field of vision, looking down on him with a piercing gaze.

"W-What did you do to me?" Vincent asked, rolling over to his hands and knees. The world spun around him, and he retched—upending the bile from his stomach.

The man snickered.

"First time being concussed, huh?"

Small droplets of blood fell from Vincent's face onto the concrete. He held his hand up to his mouth to stop the bleed.

"How about I do you a favor and explain what just happened," the man said while putting his hands back into the pockets of his hoodie and sitting lightly on Vincent's back.

"You lost...Mr. Hero."

Vincent spun around wildly to swat the man off him. His attack found nothingness, and he weakly fell to his backside.

"It was only for a split second, but you lost consciousness. I can tell you aren't used to getting hurt, but two of the hits during our fight really rocked you, right?"

Vincent remained silent—staring at the ground and gathering his composure. This guy possessed an insane amount of strength and skill. Vincent was far outmatched, although he didn't want to admit the truth of it.

"Well...you have yourself to blame for that," the man continued. "You see, both times, you decided to charge in like an idiot." He shrugged. "I just used your power against you. It's easy to predict your opponent's movement when you know exactly how they'll attack. And you, Mr. Hero…always attack in a straight line."

"Is that right?" Vincent relaxed a little, wiping the blood from his hand across the front of his singlet. It didn't seem like he would kill Vincent, and if he was going to, he probably would have done it by now.

"Say what you want about my fighting style, but even *your* attacks were weak towards the end."

The man knelt next to Vincent.

"Is that why *you're* on the ground and can't get back up?"

Try as he might, Vincent was still unable to move.

"You need more time to recover, so let's talk for a bit longer." He stood and walked over to a large piece of upended concrete. He flipped it effortlessly with one hand and sat down on the smooth surface.

Vincent didn't know what this guy was playing at, never-the-less, he wasn't in a position to deny the extra time to rest. He felt along his side —assessing whether or not his ribs were broken.

"Firstly," the man continued, without waiting for an

answer, "I've been sent to watch you and assess your strength. There's a power that's been lost to this world for a very long time, and my boss thinks that *you* might possess it."

The man played with one of the tips of his spiked maroon hair.

"Your raw strength is impressive, but not so much so that you'd normally catch our attention. Without proper training, you'd never amount to anything *that* special."

He gave Vincent a belittling smirk.

Instinctively, Vincent tried to stand back up, only to stumble and fall back down.

His legs weren't responding like they usually would.

"As for those red markings, *that's* something that *would* put you on our radar. I've fought all manner of strong opponents, but I've never seen markings like that on a Melee Meister before. So, tell me, and be honest. This wasn't the first time you've seen them, was it?"

Vincent hesitated. He didn't want to tell his guy anything—especially after all he'd done. But after a moment, his reckless curiosity outweighed his distrust.

"No." He answered carefully. "It's not the first time."

"Tell me more," the man stopped smiling, giving Vincent a cold hard stare as if he could see right through him.

Vincent smiled, his ego resurfacing along with some of his energy.

"Go to hell. I ain't telling you a damn thing. Not unless you get the Vipers out of jail."

The stranger scoffed.

"You know damn-well that I can't do that. Besides, those lowlife bastards would just go right back to their usual racket and continue holding you back. Like I said, you needed someone to free you from this place, and I've done just that."

"You piece of shit!" Vincent yelled, his voice catching on a lump in his throat. "All this... just to get to me?"

The man stood, stalking slowly toward Vincent.

"I get it; you disagree with my tactics. But tell me, Vincent, what was the alternative? Should I have killed them? They clearly couldn't be allowed to continue living here unchecked." The cold indifference in his voice turned Vincent's stomach. "Not everyone has a sudden change of heart like your friend, Badou."

Vincent's head dropped. He knew it was true, but he couldn't bring himself to endorse the man's actions. He shouldn't have come in and made these decisions on his own. He was an outsider, after all.

"That said, maybe taking them up the top of that cliff would have worked. You could have left them up there, and they'd have no way of climbing back down. It's way too far for a regular human to scale." The man gave a humorless chuckle.

"It's not too far," Vincent snapped back quietly. "There was one man who climbed that thing a long time ago."

"Then he must have been a Meister." The stranger re-affirmed.

There's that word again, Vincent thought to himself. He was beginning to understand that it referred to people with his type of power.

"Not that I owe you any explanations, but he

definitely didn't have any powers."

Vincent lowered his head.

"He was the *real* hero of the Ryuuga's," he whispered.

Vincent took a moment before locking eyes with the stranger.

"But none of that matters now. What matters is that you know that locking em up wasn't the only solution." Vincent could feel his strength returning slowly.

Just a little longer, he thought.

"So you gonna apologize and get them out, or what?"

The man responded with a steely glare—devoid of emotion.

"Haven't you been listening at all?" He asked slowly as if Vincent was a simpleton.

"Regardless of the alternatives, I did the right thing given the circumstances. Now…if you come with us, we can—"

"Don't make me laugh!" Vincent barked harshly. "It doesn't look like we'll see eye to eye on this. Maybe that's because you've only got one good one, to begin with. I said I'd kick your ass, and it's 'bout time I came good on that promise."

The man continued to look down at Vincent.

"And how do you plan on doing that?" He asked, dumbfounded by Vincent's swagger.

"Well, ya-see…as you said, it was my own strength that was hurtin' me. You've given me time to recover *and* told me what I was doin' wrong. So, the bigger question is…just how do you plan to do any damage, now that I know what *not* to do?"

Vincent gave the man a wolfish grin. The markings on his body revealed themselves again, glowing brightly. "Look at that, seems like this thing's getting easier."

Vincent put his hand on one knee and rose steadily, his breath visible in the cold night air.

They stood face-to-face yet again.

"It's gettin' late. You sure your mommy won't be worried if you're out…little boy?"

The man visibly stiffened, clenching his jaw.

Vincent placed his hand on the man's head and

ruffled his hair a little. Once Vincent found your button, it didn't matter who you were or how dire the situation; he would *always* push it.

"You can fight; I'll give you that. But you just don't have what it takes to do any real damage anymore," he added arrogantly. "Those light blasts really didn't do much."

Vincent watched as the man raised his right hand and smirked.

"Glad you think so." He announced, clicking his fingers.

Suddenly, a crushing thud vibrated throughout Vincent's entire body.

His knees buckled, and his eyes rolled into the back of his head.

The young stranger gave a breathy chuckle as an unconscious Vincent fell headfirst into the pavement. Before the red glow had faded from Vincent's skin, the man stilled. A peculiar mark glowed brightly through the back of Vincent's singlet.

He leaned over and lifted the shirt, revealing a strange

dark red symbol between Vincent's shoulder blades. The straight lines of the marking ran parallel to one another in various directions and slowly faded until they vanished entirely from sight.

"Well, I guess that confirms it." The man sucked his teeth.

"Why did the Lord have to be someone like *you*?" he hissed with disdain.

***

Vincent began to stir. His head was pounding, and he was not yet able to open his eyes.

When did I fall asleep? he wondered, staring into the blackness behind his eyelids.

A few more moments passed, and his eyes slowly fluttered open. He was still unable to move, but Vincent could feel his consciousness slowly returning. It felt as though his body was being carried.

Then, he was dropped hard onto a dusty surface with a heavy thud.

Vincent turned his head to the side, only to see a familiar sight. He was now atop the cliffs, high above the ghetto. The moon still hung high in the sky—he couldn't have been out for long.

Vincent had a case of deja-vu and wondered if this was how Badou felt earlier.

The man stood over Vincent, leaning down close.

"The fight's over; you lost…badly. I've taken you up to the top of your precious little cliff. That way, you can get some rest without being disturbed. After all, we wouldn't want people to know the great hero of the ghetto lost a fight!" he mocked, sounding almost apathetic.

"I'll give you a day to think about it, but if you decide you want to get stronger, I'll meet you here tomorrow at sunset. Who knows, maybe you can become a *real* hero and make a difference."

"W-W-Wait. What's your name?" Vincent groaned. He felt himself losing consciousness again.

The man looked blankly at Vincent for a few moments. A devilish grin crawled across his face, partly hidden by the shadows. The cross on his eyepatch caught the moonlight and appeared to emit a piercing, eerie glow.

Vincent's head fell back into the dirt. But before the darkness enveloped his mind completely, he heard a single sentence escape the man's lips.

"My name—is Zero."

Chapter Four

The dawn light spread across the Metropolitan city, preventing much of the morning sun from reaching the ghettos, which lay to the south. A few scattered rays of light crawled across the tattered town—revealing the horrendous state of the industrial district from the night before.

Badou stood at the district's edge, shadows stained beneath his eyes, wide with shock.

"VIIIIINCENT!!!"

***

Vincent's eyes twitched as his name echoed loudly through the ghetto.

With his head throbbing, and his body filled with aches and pains, Vincent slowly opened his eyes. Moaning loudly, he struggled to get up—his arms and legs reluctant to move freely.

Mornings were never kind to Vincent, but today was brutal.

"Man…I'm too young to be feeling this sore in the morning," he complained before memories of the night before struck him like a lightning bolt.

If you decide that you want to get stronger, I'll meet you up here tomorrow at sunset

"Shit," Vincent mumbled, holding the side of his head, realizing that it wasn't some terrible dream.

He had lost a fight.

Again, he heard a scream echo through the ghetto below.

"VINCENT, YOU ASSHOLE!"

Vincent gingerly walked to the edge of the cliff. He wasn't sure if it was his name being shouted into the wind, but he had an inkling. Although he couldn't see the ghetto behind the illusionary barrier, he leaned in but a little—hoping to confirm his suspicions.

Then, a sharp pain thundered through his ribs.

Vincent flinched, grabbing his side quickly, and as he did so, a portion of rock beneath his feet gave way due to the sudden shift in balance. With his body still protesting against him, and his reactions dulled, Vincent missed any opportunity to catch himself as he comically tumbled downward.

He bounced off several rocks, desperately trying to catch any natural ledges on the way down, but to no avail.

He landed at the bottom with a heavy thud—the ground cracking beneath him and the air escaping his lungs.

"Today's not gonna be my day," he mumbled, gasping for breath and closing his eyes. Several tiny pieces of rocky debris sprinkled his face from the clifftop above.

***

Vincent hobbled through the ghetto, receiving odd looks from everyone around him. They weren't used to seeing him in such a vulnerable state.

Badou's voice thundered from behind, "There you are!"

Vincent turned and received a heavy punch to his cheekbone. The lingering pains throughout his body made it near impossible for Vincent to react, and he fell backward into a pile of rubbish. The residents of the street stopped, holding their collective breath. From their eyes, Badou took down the ghetto's once-invincible monster.

Although Vincent didn't move to retaliate immediately, Badou could see the spark of anger in his eyes from within the filthy pile of trash—a rotten banana peel strewn across Vincent's face.

Badou's skin crawled, and his body winced slightly. He leaned inward as if to compensate for his actions.

"Here, man" He offered Vincent a hand up. Concern and confusion etched on his face.

As he helped Vincent up by the arm, Badou remembered the state of the Viper's hideout and let go—allowing Vincent to fall back into the rubbish behind him again.

"Oh, c'mon!" Vincent croaked out, hissing through the pain.

"Yeah, well, I thought we understood each other!" Badou bellowed.

Any onlookers who thought to linger quickly disappeared from the streets. They had seen enough of Vincent's fights to know this wouldn't end well.

"I know you can't trust me just like that, but you didn't need to trash our spot! I can't find any of the other guys either, so tell me…what did you do to them?"

Vincent pulled himself up using the wall to assist him. "Can it, will ya" he groaned.

"It wasn't me—well, okay, it was me, but not like that."

"Waddya mean?" Badou asked, shaking his head.

Vincent straightened himself, stepping out of the trash, and started walking down the street towards the industrial district—signaling for Badou to follow.

"C'mon, I'll explain on the way." He felt a bit lighter, the pains ebbing away with each step forward.

Badou, to his credit, didn't hesitate to follow Vincent. The two unlikely allies walked together through the streets as Vincent explained everything. It was no easy task, but he took their newfound truce and understanding seriously.

When they eventually arrived at the industrial district, Vincent was faced with the grim reality of the destruction left behind.

A nervous bead of sweat fell down his face as he pondered how the ghetto could look any worse.

Vincent shifted, guilt and humiliation surging through him. Not so much for the Vipers, but this district was still a part of his home...and he had unintentionally helped destroy it.

"Don't worry," Badou said, hesitantly placing a comforting hand on Vincent's shoulder. He hadn't said a word as Vincent explained what had happened. He didn't balk or shame Vincent for how the fight had ended. "It's not your fault."

Vincent looked at Badou curiously. "How did you know I was feeling guilty?"

Badou threw his head back with a hearty laugh.

"How could you not? You're used to playing the hero, not the villain. You help rebuild things, not tear em apart!" He slapped Vincent hard on the back and walked toward the debris.

"C'mon, you gonna help fix this up or not?"

***

Later that afternoon, Vincent and Badou had finally gone their separate ways. They had spent the entire day trying to straighten bent pipes and beams, reattaching previously connected supports, and clearing away debris.

Vincent walked through the ghetto streets with his hands in his pockets, looking down at the ground. Reflecting on all the work they had just done; he was glad that they could fix most of the damage.

Although he knew that Zero was partly responsible for the destruction, Vincent couldn't help the guilt that crept through him, all too aware that he had initiated the fight in the first place.

He replayed Badou's words from the alleyway the day before. *You just had to dive in and recklessly attack. You know that temper of yours is what makes you predictable.* He then thought back to the similar advice given to him by Zero.

Looks like Badou's not the only one who needs to learn how to do things differently.

A faint smile appeared on his face. The ache in his chest eased slightly. Finally, he and Badou had formed some sort of amicable relationship.

"All it took was a literal change in perspective…and for me to get my ass kicked," he chuckled.

Vincent looked up at the Starfall cliffs as the sun began to set. They passed in and out of view between the buildings on his way home.

"True strength, huh?"

Vincent stopped and darted back towards the

industrial district with a determined gleam in his eyes. When he arrived, Vincent found Badou sitting in front of a bin fire, with several boxes piled around him.

"What's with the boxes?" Vincent asked.

Badou looked behind him and slapped the side of the nearest container.

"Oh, I thought you went home for the day. This is all the food and supplies that me and the guys stole over the last few months."

Vincent raised an eyebrow.

"You leavin' or something?" He asked.

Badou leaned back again, resting his outstretched hands on the concrete behind him.

"Nah, but I don't need an empty snake nest." he chuckled.

"I dunno, you got a lot of space here now. Why not make the most of it? Besides, this place finally has enough room for your ego," Vincent joked. It had been so long since he could play earnestly with anyone. It felt nice to have a friend, and he wanted to preserve this moment. He hesitated—second-guessing what he had come to say.

Badou leaned forward and hopped back to his feet.

"You and that Zero guy trashed this place pretty good, but you're right. It's still got plenty of room and shelter…shelter the people of the ghetto could use."

"And the boxes?" Vincent quizzed.

"I'm gonna open em up and offer all of it back first thing tomorrow morning. My way of saying sorry, I guess."

Vincent was touched, and he smiled genuinely for the first time in years.

"Besides…" Badou stoked the fire with a block of broken wood. "You have somewhere else you need to be, right?"

Vincent nodded. With embers sparking into the air from the fire, Badou turned to face Vincent—offering him an outstretched hand.

Vincent chuckled softly, meeting Badou with a firm handshake.

"Thanks. But hey, if I find out you're causing trouble, I'll tell everyone how you pissed yourself!"

"Yeah? And I'll tell everyone how you got your ass kicked by a man with only one eye!"

Vincent gazed unflinchingly at Badou. He'd seen the worst of this man over the years and found it hard to suddenly place such a tremendous trust in him.

Yet to Vincent's surprise, there was no deceit in Badou's eyes…not this time.

It reminded Vincent of the look Badou used to have before he got caught up in all the gang activity. Back when the Vipers' Fang, Badou, was just a teenager who liked to tinker with his motorcycle and work out. In those days, a much younger Vincent used to idolize the ruffian—desperate to be accepted by the 'big kid on the block.'

Vincent held Badou's gaze for a moment longer before letting go of the handshake.

He smiled and turned to walk away…lifting his hand in farewell.

"Look after everyone, will ya?! Believe it or not, you can be a cool guy when you're not acting like a jackass. Some of the kids round here might even look up to you over time. They might want to be your friend, so try not to treat people like crap just because they're a little different, okay?"

Vincent's departing words hit Badou with a feeling of sudden realization. He smiled broadly and called back.

"Yeah, you're right...you never know when one of em might grow up to be the guy who saves this place!"

Vincent's face was covered in shadows, and a tear fell from beneath the brim of Vincent's hat. It rolled around an amused smirk as he turned a corner—disappearing from Badou's sight.

"Jackass."

***

Running as fast as he could towards the base of the cliffs, Vincent replayed Zero's words again: *If you decide that you want to get stronger, I'll meet you up here again tomorrow at sunset.* Without any more doubts or loose ends to tend to, Vincent was ecstatic to embark on a new journey. His mind was overflowing with possibilities. Sure, that Zero guy was a jerk...but he was strong—much stronger. If he could befriend Badou, maybe he could start fresh with Zero.

Vincent bounced his way back up the steep ridge—trying to beat the setting sun.

***

Just before the last light had left the sky, Vincent arrived at the peak. But there was nobody to be seen.

"Zero!" he called.

A few minutes passed by, but there was nothing.

Vincent paced back and forth, wondering if Zero was late. The excitement began to transition into worry. He didn't want to go back now. He was finally ready.

Then, something caught his eye—something that replaced all of Vincent's newfound positivity with frustration, anger, and contempt.

There, in the dirt, was a message:

A sudden wave of exhaustion hit Vincent, coupled with a simultaneous burning desire for unbridled violence.

"I hate him *so* much!" Vincent growled, focusing on the crudely drawn picture.

"And what does he mean, *don't die?*"

Vincent kicked his feet through the message and faced the forest, stretching his arms and bending side-to-side in preparation.

"I'll show him. I'll get there in ONE day." he confidently proclaimed.

Vincent readied himself for a mad dash forward. But before doing so, he paused and looked around at the large, expansive forest before him. He cocked his head to one side. "Wait...which way is south?"

Feeling a little embarrassed, Vincent stood back up and began pacing back and forth, cursing loudly. However, as he did so, he spied another message written in the dirt on the far side of the clearing.

He stormed over and looked down.

"I'LL KILL HIM!" Vincent roared aloud as all the birds in the surrounding trees scattered.

"Okay, let's try this again." He held his breath, calming himself slightly.

Vincent held his foot over the grass…just as he had done every day at sunset. Only this time, he exhaled slowly and put his weight down, stepping into the forest toward his future.

***

It wasn't long before Vincent came across a large wall painted in the same colors as the ones in Ryuuga. It even looked similar to the one separating the ghetto from the Metropolis. But to his surprise, the wall before him now seemed far less formidable…even for an average human.

Vincent theorized that it was probably more to keep animals out rather than humans—while also marking the area as private property.

The dense forest had grown close to the wall—almost camouflaging it entirely, and giving off a post-apocalyptic vibe. Clearly, nobody was maintaining it.

Vincent leapt over the boundary of concrete and metal easily, landing lightly on the other side. He dusted himself off and looked up to find a deep thicket of overgrown grass, vines, and large trees that seemed to stretch out for an eternity.

This was the unknown, and it made him uneasy. In contrast to its lush beauty, the forest also carried a menacing and dangerous aura.

Shaking this feeling aside, Vincent couldn't wait to experience the new world before him.

All he had to do, was cross the Starfall Forest.

<u>Chapter Five</u>

Vincent had traveled as far and fast as he could on the afternoon of his departure before reluctantly stopping to rest against an old, fallen tree after night had set in. He couldn't relax or stop his knee from bouncing from impatience. He had vowed to reach Chedda in a single day, and he wasn't about to let Zero win again. However, exhaustion and fatigue from the past two days quickly pulled him under into a fitful sleep.

***

As dawn broke, a variety of colorful birds sang softly, whispering to one another, and small creatures scurried through the undergrowth into the shadows. However, this peace and tranquility were quickly disturbed by thundering footsteps as Vincent tore through the jungle of weeds and plant-life like a man possessed.

It was Vincent's first time outside of the Ryuuga prefecture, and the world was entirely new to him. He ran headlong into the wild abyss with passion and enthusiasm at the helm. Despite the burning desire to cover ground quickly, Vincent couldn't help but frequently stop whenever a strange-looking bug, a peculiar rock, or even an unfamiliar color caught his attention. Each distraction, no matter how innocent or childlike, only further diverted Vincent from his direction to the south.

After a full day of exploration, the sun hung low in the sky as he reached the painful conclusion that he was well and truly lost.

Cursing and grumbling, Vincent tried to reorient

himself, retracing his steps before settling at a nearby lake that led to a large waterfall. His eyes trailed the flight of an insect with fluorescent blue wings that left a turquoise trail of light behind as it zipped by. The small creature hovered over the stream, setting itself down on the water's surface for a brief moment. Distracted yet again, Vincent leaned in with a naïve curiosity. As his nose approached the tiny, winged creature, a large fish with six glowing yellow eyes quickly burst upward and gobbled up the insect in an instant—dousing his face.

Vincent's frustration was a constant simmer beneath his skin. He felt silly for being so gung-ho, but his pride demanded that he finish what he started. He wanted to prove something to Zero…and himself.

Vincent wiped his face on the front of his dirty singlet as he marveled at the cascading body of water. Orange and red light crept through the foliage of the treetops above, dancing on the rippling water's edge. Vincent slowly rose to his feet. How could it be sunset already? He had barely made any progress, and he was still lost in this godforsaken place.

He scowled, remembering Zero's smug face and the note scratched into the ground.

South is this way, Moron!

Puzzled and scratching his head frantically, Vincent closed his eyes thinking back to the direction of the sunset the day before. *If the sun was to my right yesterday*—Vincent's eyes snapped open, and he smirked— impressed by his self-appointed brilliance.

This way must be south! He assured, squatting down low and launching himself high into the air. Vincent was dazzled by the forest's beauty from this angle and height, but he couldn't see anything that resembled a pathway or a town in the distance.

"Holy crap!" Vincent exclaimed. "Zero was serious when he said it would take two days!" Landing hard at the water's edge in a crouch, Vincent stretched his legs and arms. There was no way he was stopping for another night.

However, the jump had given Vincent an idea.

Prepping himself like an athlete at the starting blocks for a sprint, Vincent placed his hands on the ground and braced his legs, before darting forward at top speed. He leapt upward with all his might—launching himself into the sky yet again. With the momentum catapulting him forward, Vincent covered a great distance as he sailed high above the treetops. The woodland vista was a blur beneath his feet, and he soon descended back beneath the foliage, landing with a thud and cracking the ground underfoot.

Perfect! He thought to himself, mentally patting himself on the back.

He might be there before daybreak at this rate, at least.

Each time Vincent propelled himself upwards, it brought him closer and closer to Zero.

Vincent's confidence surged as he repeatedly soared through the afternoon sky. But as the sun set, the forest became engulfed in darkness, and landing had become increasingly difficult. He had no visibility of his surroundings and no time to adjust or prepare for the uneven terrain below as he fell. Vincent's 'brilliant' idea was becoming less brilliant with each clumsy stumble or slip.

He considered running the rest of the way, but as he descended one final time, his foot landed on something soft.

A shrieking howl permeated through the darkness, blanketing the forest, as Vincent toppled over. Groaning, he got back to his feet, dusting himself off. It was likely that he had killed the poor creature. The sheer velocity of his descent would have shattered its body completely. The least he could do was bury the poor thing.

***

Very few creatures made their way into the ghetto, but when they did, Vincent went out of his way to care for any strays he found.

Vincent could just make out several large shapes ahead as his eyes adjusted to the darkness of the forest. Deep, menacing growls emanated from the shadows around him, and Vincent backed away cautiously. He looked around, spotting a clearing where the moonlight illuminated a small portion of the open area. Vincent began to run, but he heard the gallop of several pairs of heavy footsteps pursuing closely behind as he did so.

Having reached the clearing, he quickly spun around to prepare himself.

The thunderous footsteps slowed—careful not to reveal themselves while staying within the shadows of the tree line. Although Vincent was aware that many creatures now surrounded him, something large was approaching from the back of the pack. He could feel a dark power emanating from the beast, and the hairs on the back of his neck rose.

He steeled himself in anticipation.

Slowly, a massive scaled, black paw with razor-sharp claws caught the moonlight as the beast sauntered out from the shadows. It was an enormous demonic dog-like creature, each leg as thick as Vincent's entire body. It was roughly twelve feet in length, with a muscular form and dark coarse fur covering most of its body.

A long tail, filled with scales and a massive tuft of hair at its tip, followed lazily behind the beast as it crept forward. All other features paled compared to this behemoth's terrifying long, sharp horn that protruded from its forehead.

This creature…was a HELLHOUND.

A terrifying, nocturnal monster that hunted in large numbers, with a single alpha leading each pack.

Vincent went pale; he was terrified at the sight of the beast.

Quickly eyeing the trees around him, eight slightly smaller hellhounds stepped out of the shadows.

The alpha let out a blood-curdling howl that pierced Vincent's head. He covered his ears from the piercing shriek as one of the creatures leapt toward him.

The hellhound swiped at Vincent with deadly precision, missing him by a hair's breadth, slicing open the side of his singlet and leaving a small gash in his side.

Vincent looked down, stunned.

How could he be bleeding from the claw of a beast when knives, swords, or even a gun couldn't pierce his flesh?

Vincent's stomach dropped as nervousness and fear prickled his skin.

He had no idea how to fight these monsters, but he bared his teeth at the beasts around him in warning.

Strangely, the last part of Zero's note flashed in his mind. *Don't Die.*

What a smartass. Vincent thought to himself.

But if he were going down, it certainly wouldn't be without a fight.

Another hellhound leapt out, swiping at Vincent's leg, testing him, and attempting to cripple and incapacitate his movements. Vincent jumped, easily avoiding the attack, only for another hound to swipe out from behind. Despite Vincent's lightning-fast reflexes, these demonic-looking beasts were intelligent and hunting in a pattern. All eight of the smaller hellhounds were working together as if with one mind to bring Vincent down.

Meanwhile, the Alpha stood silently…watching. Its lips quivered to reveal several rows of large white fangs, and a thick string of pungent drool hung from its mouth.

It was savoring the hunt, barely able to contain its anticipation to tear into Vincent's blood-soaked flesh.

With each attack more vicious than the last, Vincent dodged and flailed relentlessly. As he did so, the circle of beasts around him grew smaller—greatly reducing his maneuverability.

It wasn't looking good. Sweat dripped from his brow as Vincent tried to calm himself.

Pushing away the fear and panic rising in his chest, he took a deep breath. He would have to go on the offensive if he was to make it through this alive.

A hellhound moved toward him, but this time Vincent lunged forward, dodging the beast's claws and delivering a heavy blow to its face.

Vincent could hardly believe how hard the creature's skull was. His fist was throbbing from the impact, but his attack had sent the hellhound soaring.

The rest of the pack jumped back from him—wary.

This was his chance. Vincent made a break for it, rushing through a narrow gap between the beasts and sprinting into the darkness at top speed. He had no idea which way to go, but given the circumstances, he didn't care. It wasn't likely that he wouldn't be able to hide, but maybe, just maybe, he could get to higher ground.

Vincent's body was seizing as he ran. He was already

exhausted from refusing to rest throughout the day. He could no longer run at his top speed, and he could feel the pack closing in behind him.

Several smaller hellhounds began to overtake his pace, keeping a tight formation to surround their prey.

Then, in a split second, Vincent veered off to the right and straight into one of the hellhounds—knocking it off balance and delivering a heavy blow to its face.

"That's two down!" Vincent exclaimed.

Another leapt out of the darkness and attacked.

Vincent jumped backward and awaited the inevitable back-attack. He turned in anticipation, and sure enough, there was one of the devilish canines, mid-jump in his direction. Its boisterous roar was cut short by Vincent smashing his fist into its open jaw, shattering bone, and sending its massive tusk-like teeth across the forest floor.

"That's three!"

"Annnnd four!" he jeered as another beast was taken out with a lightning-fast elbow to the temple.

Vincent smiled from ear to ear—confident that he had

figured out their attack patterns.

This sudden outburst of happiness would have appeared psychotic to an observer. Here he was, in unfamiliar territory with several apex predators trying to feast on his flesh, yet Vincent couldn't help but relish the challenge. Beating an enemy with so much power was exhilarating.

The remaining hellhounds scattered, darting throughout the forest, and circled Vincent as they ran at terrifying speeds. Vincent's eyes could barely keep up with them, and they each let loose a blood-curdling howl. The high-pitched halo of noise painfully blasted into Vincent's eardrums. Disorientated and off-balance, he stumbled while holding his head.

Suddenly, the gigantic alpha burst through the canopy overhead, landing next to Vincent with a heavy thud. It surged forward, scooping its head down and back up again violently.

Shock rippled through Vincent as a small stream of blood trickled down his side. His eyes wide, Vincent shuddered, looking down at the alpha's horn skewered through his left shoulder. The blood-crazed hellhound let out a tremendous guttural roar—lifting its head and waving Vincent's body around like a victory flag.

Pain like he had never felt before radiated through Vincent's body as he screamed in both terror and agony. He grabbed the ivory horn with shaking hands while a steady river of blood poured from the gaping wound through his fingers. The slick red wetness ran across the alpha's harsh brow, settling into the monster's mouth. Piercing red eyes bore into Vincent's as the beast drank deeply, closing its eyes and losing itself to the bloodlust. Suddenly, a red glow illuminated the vermillion canine's face from above—its triumph premature.

Vincent's eyes were wide, beaming a bright white, as the intricate red glowing patterns scorched into his body lit up the surrounding area.

For a brief moment, Vincent appeared more menacing than the alpha that had impaled him.

The beast looked up frightfully just as Vincent's fist hammered down, shattering through the giant horn. The forest echoed with the hellhound's pain-filled wail. It recoiled, pawing at its face in distress.

With the horn still lodged in his shoulder, Vincent landed heavily on the ground, blood spilling around his feet.

The rage that had taken over had quickly subsided, and his mind was clear again. However, Vincent had lost a great deal of blood. The beast was far too formidable; even in his weakened state, there was no way that he could defeat it.

His only option was to flee.

A trail of blood lined the forest floor behind Vincent as he ran. The red marks across his body began to flicker and fade along with most of his fleeting strength.

The rest of the pack gave chase, and Vincent's vision started to fade. He couldn't catch his breath, and it was getting more and more labored.

Suddenly, Vincent's legs gave out beneath him, and he came down hard, chin first into the dirt.

The pack of hellhounds surrounded him again, tightening their perimeter, making a single space for the alpha to step through. The injured behemoth inched closer, its massive frame looming over Vincent's bloodied body.

Vincent closed his eyes; this was it.

The beast hung its head over the nape of Vincent's neck, ready to strike.

Vincent reflected upon his recent trend of near-death experiences. After seventeen years of feeling indestructible, suddenly, he would face his mortality twice in three days.

The irony was not lost on him.

He was not ready to die, and he desperately tried to figure a way out of this mess. After so many new experiences in such a short time, his life had finally started to change.

Hope wasn't just some fleeting dream anymore.

Vincent's mind scrambled, desperately searching for anything, anyone who could help him. He uttered a single breathless word, "help," but it was barely a whisper.

Then, out of the darkness, he heard a shout, followed by a bright orange light that blanketed the forest floor.

Vincent lifted his head, but all he could see was the distorted image of a figure waving what looked like fire.

Vincent's lips quivered—attempting to form words, but before his fate was clear, the world went black.

Vincent had lost consciousness.

<u>Chapter Six</u>

Visions of red water swelled through Vincent's subconscious.

A strange black cloud spread through the crimson reservoir. Terrified and tortured screams echoed in the depths, pleading for their lives. Several black tendrils formed in the mist, reaching out, constricting around the throat of a limp muscular blonde-haired man. Suddenly, his green eyes shot open in terror.

***

Vincent snapped awake, sweating after another one of his strange dreams. But this was the first time he'd had this one, and his head was already aching.

He found himself inside a dank cave, with a large entrance a few feet away.

The sound of the wind rustling through the treetops, coupled with the harmonies of nearby birds, told Vincent that he was still somewhere in the forest. Or at least nearby.

"Yo…. you up, tough guy?"

Vincent's eyes looked over to where he had heard the voice. He attempted to rise, wincing at the sharp pain in his shoulder. Looking up, he saw the silhouette of a broad male leaning against one of the cave walls.

"W-Who are you? And how did I get here?" Vincent grunted.

"Jet's the name, my man—listen, you got a hole in your shoulder, so be careful." He walked over to Vincent, offering a rough stone cup with green fluid pooling inside.

"Here, drink this. It's a special remedy I use to treat pain and infections. You've been out cold since last night, so downing some of this stuff will help. I did what I could to patch you up, but you need to get that injury seen by a doctor as soon as possible."

Vincent held the cup, eyeing the liquid suspiciously.

"Truth be told, I was going to try and carry you to Chedda if you didn't come good by morning. But you heal *real* fast! The hole is still there, but the bleeding stopped pretty quickly. Your temperature had broken, so I decided to let you rest and see how things panned out."

Vincent looked down and saw that his chest and shoulder had been strapped up with bandages and treated with some basic first aid. The hole in his shoulder was packed with what looked to be some sort of herbal concoction.

"Uh, thanks," he replied.

Vincent studied Jet suspiciously. Large black dreadlocks fell past his chest, where a strange ring dangled from a chain around his neck. Vincent's gaze caught on the thick, golden bracers that encircled Jet's wrists and ankles. As he moved about the cave, they glinted in the afternoon light beaming through the entrance of the cave.

"Where am I?" Vincent asked.

"You're still in Starfall. You're lucky to be alive, bro," Jet looked like he was holding in a grin. "Only a moron would travel through this place at night. Hellhounds are nocturnal and ruthless killers…and the alphas certainly aren't anything to sneeze at."

Vincent's eye twitched at being called a moron, annoyingly reminding him of Zero.

"Uh-huh," Vincent exhaled sharply as he sat up slowly, covertly examining the surface of the cave walls.

"So, how did you find me? Are we close to this *Chedda* place or something?" Vincent hedged. He'd met very few people in his life who would save a total stranger without expecting something in return. Vincent was grateful, although he was used to being the savior and never the one being saved.

Jet made his way to a nearby window in the cave, looking out. Vincent watched him as he closed his eyes, took a deep breath, and sighed. The peaceful expression on Jet's face surprised him.

"I love nature," Jet said, his eyes focused out the window. "I like to travel about and camp outdoors," he exclaimed happily, turning to Vincent. Jet's eyes were bright and earnest as he continued.

"When I heard your screams last night, I came running and found you just as you were about to become hellhound food. They hate fire, you feel me? Next time you're traveling these parts at night, carry some fire around, and they should leave you be. That said, if a hellhound spots an opportunity to get you away from the fire, they'll take it in a second. Anyways, I spooked em off and carried you here. Their pack should still be nearby. They stalk their prey relentlessly until you leave their territory, so they'll move in again come nightfall."

Vincent's eyes traveled the cave walls again. Although he'd never been inside a cave before, something wasn't right about its design. He knew what rock looked like, and the formation of the interior surfaces looked far too smooth.

Slowly, Vincent stood up from his makeshift bed of stone and dirt. Stretching his legs out, he staggered towards the light outside—careful not to turn his back on Jet.

Jet seemed kind enough, but old habits die hard.

"Where are you trying to go, friend?" Jet inquired, following him out of the cave.

Squinting, Vincent's eyes adjusted to the warm rays of light piercing through the foliage above. He pondered how honest he could be. As he took another step, Vincent lost his balance and tripped over the uneven terrain, falling to the ground and spilling his drink deliberately to avoid Jet's suspicion.

"Woah, easy there, my man." Jet kneeled to help Vincent up.

"I think I've just gotten a little turned around." Vincent grimaced, slowly rising back to his feet. "Did you say Chedda was nearby?"

"Yeah, brother…actually, it's not too far at all," Jet answered with a sincere smile that put Vincent's mind at ease, if only by a little.

"Just head that way for about an hour." Jet pointed towards the forest helpfully.

He threw Vincent his blood-stained singlet that had been folded nearby. As Vincent slipped it back on, wincing slightly, he smiled gratefully at Jet.

"Thanks for the help, man, I owe you one, but I gotta go."

Jet casually waved off his thanks as they exited the cave together. "No stress, my dude. You right to get there on your own?" he asked.

"Yeah, I should be right. Thanks again" Vincent tentatively extended a hand to Jet.

Without hesitating, Jet reciprocated. "Take care, man."

Over Jet's shoulder, Vincent noticed a patch of dried blood staining the exterior of one of the cave walls. His eyes narrowed, and he bid Jet farewell without giving away his growing suspicions.

Vincent turned and started towards Chedda. He glanced around to get his bearings and noticed a black scorch mark on the ground nearby. He looked around quickly, now noticing several claw marks etched into the trunks of the surrounding trees.

Vincent stilled. This was the exact spot where he had fallen last night.

Dark as it may be, Vincent was certain that there was no cave here the night before.

Vincent spun around. "Hey, can you tell m—" Jet had vanished, and there was no sign of the cave that had been there seconds ago.

Vincent looked around and rubbed his eyes, questioning his sanity for the briefest moment. Dumbfounded, he wondered if he'd ingested something illicit during his slumber. He called out to Jet, but there was nothing. Vincent shook his head, trying to clear his mind. He turned to take a few steps, but as he did so, his foot connected with the small stone cup still laying on the ground—a few drops of the green liquid still beading the rim.

Vincent was torn. He wanted to investigate this strange, almost other-worldly experience, but he could tell it was nearing mid-afternoon. There wasn't much time left in the day, and he was concerned about his injured shoulder. Vincent wasn't sure he'd be in any condition to fight if something foul was afoot.

"I guess it can't be helped," Vincent whispered to himself while scratching the back of his head in frustration.

Meanwhile, a figure loomed high above in the treetops—watching as Vincent reluctantly turned and continued on his journey.

***

A little over an hour later, Vincent found himself beneath a large wooden sign hanging from two tiki posts, each carved into decorative horses.

Etched calligraphy in the sign that connected them were the following words: *Welcome to Chedda.*

Vincent walked curiously through the small town. Despite his injuries, he couldn't help but feel somewhat refreshed. Chedda was the first town he'd ever seen outside the Ryuuga Ghetto. Marveling at the rustic décor, Vincent couldn't help but take in every strange building decorated in a horse motif. Before long, he spotted a large, single-story building with a rusted and scratched horseshoe hanging above the entrance. Beneath, a sign read *The Thirsty Horse.*

Curious, Vincent entered through the swinging wooden saloon doors. It was unlike anything he had ever seen.

Striding towards the bar, Vincent pulled up a stool, shrewdly studying a stocky, bearded barkeep. Bearing the stigmata often created more problems than it was worth, so Vincent lowered his head to hide the black ring encircling his neck.

"What is this place?" he asked, staring at the battered stage in the corner, then at a group of men playing cards at a table nearby.

The barkeep smiled jovially at Vincent, taking him by surprise.

"Welcome to The Thirsty Horse, your *mane* stay for a *stable* drink! I can make any refreshment you want…*spur* of the moment." Vincent was utterly confused by literally everything the man had just said.

"Uhhhhhh, what's good?" He asked dubiously.

Scratching his beard thoughtfully, the barkeep replied, "Everyone has their own tastes, but you look like a man who would like our house-made smokey sour beer."

"Sure?" Vincent replied, his high inflection making his response sound more like a question than an answer.

The barkeep tilted a long glass and poured a cold frosty beer, sliding it across the table to Vincent, smiling expectantly. "That'll be nine-fifty."

Vincent realized that some form of payment was required from him, but the thought had slipped his mind before ordering. He searched his pockets but had no idea why; knowing full well that he had no money.

"It's on me," a man called out.

Leaning against a nearby pole, the man placed a few crisp bills onto the bar and signaled to the barkeep.

"Thanks," Vincent breathed, slightly relieved.

He subtly scanned the well-dressed gentleman. A green gem hung from a chain around his neck, and scars marred the otherwise striking features of his face. A clean cross-shaped scar was visible on his left cheek, and a vertical cut ran down across his right eye.

"So, you must be Vincent Clyne. I've heard a lot about you," he drawled.

Vincent choked, mid-sip from his very first beer. The rest of his mouthful sprayed all over the unimpressed barkeep.

Mortified, Vincent sat there, his mouth agape as beer dripped down the large man's face.

The two locked eyes uncomfortably. Vincent shifted but didn't dare blink.

The young man sauntered up behind Vincent and hung his arm over his shoulder like they were old buddies.

"I thought your throat was a little…*hoarse*! Sorry about my friend, *neighbor, but* surely there's no need to look so…*long* in the face?" The barkeep stood there silently for a few moments before breaking his stern expression and erupting into a hearty laugh.

He wiped the beer from his face with a washcloth and continued cleaning the bar.

"I don't get it," Vincent whispered, looking between

the barkeep and the handsome stranger draped over his shoulder.

"Chedda's famous for breeding horses. Nearly everything here is horse themed, and our large friend there really seems to enjoy a pun or two," he explained, gesturing for Vincent to finish his drink.

"Uh, um…so you're the guy I'm s'posed to meet?" Vincent asked, downing the frothy beverage.

"The name's Agito. Listen, I'll be your guide until we reach our destination, and we've got a long way to go. Zero tells me you have a bit of an attitude—"

Vincent shot up quickly, his stool toppling backward, disrupting the other patrons as they drank. "Where is that bastard? I have a bone to pick with him!"

Agito appraised Vincent's rough veneer, pausing on the bloodied bandage beneath his singlet. He cleared his throat.

"Ahem. As I was saying…Zero tells me you have a bit of an attitude."

Agito held out his hand, and a fire erupted from his palm—extinguishing suddenly with a flick of his wrist.

"So, if you just shut up and do as I say, we won't have any problems…you got that?"

Vincent's eyes widened. No one else had witnessed the flames, and even if they did, they certainly didn't react.

"How'd you do that?!" Vincent asked aggressively.

Agito chuckled. "There's a lot of things in this world you haven't seen, my friend." Agito scrunched up his nose, slightly disgusted, "One of which, I suspect, is a shower."

As Agito led them from the bar, Vincent looked down at his grubby attire and sniffed himself, flinching at his own offensive body odor.

Agito strode purposefully through Chedda, with Vincent struggling to keep up and easily distracted by the unfamiliar sights and smells. He bombarded Agito with questions along the way, but they fell on deaf ears.

Frustrated, Vincent watched Agito's long brown braided hair sway behind him. His brilliant emerald-green gem, encased by a golden harness, caught the sunlight with each step. He was attractive despite the scars, catching the eye of every woman he passed.

Vincent took a few quick paces to catch up.

"How'd you get the scars?" he asked—his social etiquette clearly lacking.

Agito slowed, stopping beneath a large tree soon after the edge of town.

"Yo!" he yelled out, looking up.

A mysterious stranger suddenly appeared on a nearby branch, as if teleported into existence. Dressed like a ninja, the person was donned in black, with white arm wraps and light armor around the chest and shoulders. A black hood with cat ears and a small, half-mask obscured their identity and gender, while a long tail with a razor-sharp claw on its tip wrapped itself around the branch.

"What the hell? Where'd he come from?!" Vincent shouted.

"Hey Kira, think you can patch up our new friend here?" Agito signaled toward Vincent. Kira disappeared, reappearing behind Vincent in a fraction a second, both startling and aggravating him.

"Hold still," Kira murmured.

Unsure of what to make of this, Vincent looked to Agito for answers. Agito smiled as Kira held out both hands over Vincent's shoulder.

"Hey, what are you doing?" He asked, trying in vain to see behind him.

A soft, yellow light emanated from Kira's hands, and a strange warmth spread into Vincent's shoulder. After a moment, the pain began to ease until it was barely an ache to Vincent's utter astonishment.

His eyes widened. "What the hell?"

Rotating his arm around freely, he tried to make sense of what he'd witnessed—what he'd felt.

Kira had already disappeared from behind him and then reappeared next to Agito.

"Careful," Kira warned, in barely more than a whisper, "All I did was close the wound. The internal damage is still very much there, but it should do until you reach Pulse".

"Pulse?" Vincent repeated, looking up from his shoulder. He'd never heard of it. Agito grinned and patted Vincent on his good shoulder.

"I'll explain on the way," he laughed.

***

Dusk had set in, and they made their way by foot through the thinned bushland.

Lost in thought on all that had occurred since he had left the ghetto, Vincent didn't notice when he could smell and taste salt in the air. It was only when he started to hear a bizarre watery noise carried on the wind, that he looked up to see the end of the bushland not far ahead. Both eager and alert for any danger, Vincent followed Agito and Kira through the trees.

Before them was a blanket of pure, white sand; beyond that was a sparkling blue body of water stretched out as far as the eye could see. Vincent's breath caught. It was the most incredible sight he had ever experienced. The breathtaking cobalt ocean and the sea breeze gently massaging his face overloaded Vincent's senses.

"I-I-I…I don't…I don't understand. What is this place?" he asked.

His eyes were wide; he didn't want to miss a moment.

Agito smiled at Vincent's childlike wonder. "It's the

ocean."

Vincent's brow furrowed. "So…Zero's out there?"

"Moron…"

Vincent spun, frantically searching for the owner of the disembodied voice. Agito barked with laughter, and Kira let out a faint chuckle.

Vincent growled; he couldn't see anyone, and there was nowhere to hide across the white dunes or in the ocean's swell. Then, out of the corner of his eye, Vincent spied a blue shimmer of light at the water's edge. Suddenly, a sleek boat that had been invisible came into view. Sitting on the stern, with a superior smirk spread across his face, was Zero.

Chapter Seven

Vincent's expression darkened. He was ready for a fight, and Zero was clearly enjoying his irritation.

"What the hell is that? *Where* was it…AND YOU hiding?" Vincent demanded, grinding his teeth. "Is this like that insect you put on my hat?"

Zero threw back his head and laughed as he stood from the top of the stern, looking down his nose at Vincent.

"Insect? You mean the BUG that I placed on you, right?" he drawled, jumping gracefully from the boat, barely making an impact or indentation on the sand.

Every word Zero spoke sent waves of frustration and anger through Vincent—although he did not know why. Nevertheless, Vincent wanted nothing more than to wipe that infuriating smirk clean off his face.

Zero continued his explanation.

"We have technology that hides anything made from a special metal we developed. It's like the illusionary barrier around the ghetto, military-grade, but ours is better." Zero looked briefly back at the boat with pride.

"It can even hide people if they're touching it, but they have to either be incredibly still or concealed entirely."

He paused in front of Vincent.

The intense rage that Zero brought out of him had quickly ebbed; the technology before his eyes piquing his curiosity instead.

"You…gotta be joking," Vincent exclaimed in wonder. "That's incredible!"

Zero scoffed at his remark.

"Nah, the real joke was that pitiful display you put on in Starfall."

Vincent's frustration returned in force. He locked eyes with Zero, and he curled his hands into tightly wound fists.

"I mean, I figured you'd be stupid enough to travel at night, but to think you'd literally stumble on a hellhound pack—AND that you would only put down a few of them."

A smug look sprawled across Zero's face, and he slapped Vincent on his injured shoulder—knowing full well that he wasn't fully healed. "Frankly, I'm disappointed."

Vincent clenched his jaw to hide his wince, refusing to give Zero the satisfaction. He met his gaze with a fierce intensity.

"What the hell is that s'posed to mean?" Vincent hissed, "How did you know all that? Were you there?!"

Zero's smile widened as he looked off into the distance. He pretended to take a moment to appreciate the fine weather, but this too was just another way to belittle Vincent—and Vincent knew this.

"That's right; I was there. I was there when you saw my message in the dirt. I was there when you got yourself lost by looking at every bloody thing that caught your eye, and I was there when you made the idiotic decision to jump your way through the forest after dark and landed on that hellhound."

Zero laughed heartily, and he turned back to face Vincent.

"I mean, I wanted to laugh so hard that I almost gave myself awa—."

THWACK

Zero fell backward into the sand with Vincent standing over him.

"Looks like you don't see quite so much when I smack you on your blind side, you one-eyed asshole!"

Zero pulled himself up, barely able to contain his still ever-present smile. There was no hint that Vincent's punch had any effect at all.

"Settle down, slugger. You were never in any real

danger."

Vincent's eye twitched.

"ARE YOU KIDDING ME?!" Vincent screamed at the top of his lungs—flailing his hands out. His body shook with anxiety and anger.

"I GOT A HOLE IN MY DAMN SHOULDER! YOU COULD HAVE HELPED, BUT YOU JUST SAT THERE WATCHING?!" ARE YOU BLIND OR JUST HEARTLESS?"

Zero raised an eyebrow and sighed.

"I see more than you think…" he replied calmly, dusting the sand from his clothes.

"Okay, you got your little shot in, and you blew off some steam. But now we need to get going."

"No," Vincent interjected aggressively.

"You've had a problem with me since the second we met, and I'm sick of your attitude."

"My attitude? That's rich!" Zero's expression turned cold, and his piercing gaze set Vincent back, if only a little.

"You're a sheltered brat who acts like you've suffered

so damned much…when in reality, you've seen nothing of the real hardships this world has to offer. Hell, you've not even seen the world outside of that pathetic little dust bowl! You seem to think you're this big hero who has no friends solely because you have powers that others don't?"

Zero reared his head back and scoffed.

"Heh, don't make me laugh! Did you ever think for a second that it might not be your strength that pushes people away…but maybe your rotten personality?"

Stunned, Vincent managed to utter only a few meager words: "You don't know me."

"Give me a break." Zero retaliated.

"People are the most honest when they think they're alone, and I watched you for a full week. Then, when I finally decided it was time to reveal myself, I goaded you and gave you every opportunity to rise above the situation. To show me something…ANYTHING to indicate that you're worthy of becoming the Melee Lord. You're brash, temperamental, cocky, and stubborn, just to name a few. Don't project your inadequacies onto others and then tell yourself it's because you're special."

And there it was, the reason Zero seemed to get under his skin so easily.

Despite being cold and unfeeling, Zero was laying bare all the insecurities that Vincent had buried deep within himself. Vincent's chin fell to his chest and his eyes into the sand.

But Zero gave Vincent's clear embarrassment no reprieve.

"Look, you can throw a tantrum all you like, but you'll not land another punch. Like it or not, Vincent, you're the new Lord, and you're coming with us."

He turned his back on Vincent and walked to the boat without another word.

Still ashamed and embarrassed, Vincent struggled to put one foot in front of the other.

Why was he going along with these people? Clearly, he was not wanted. They were just completing a mission, and he was their target.

Lost in self-pity and deprecating thought, Vincent suddenly felt a light pat on his shoulder.

It was Agito.

"Hey man, look, don't worry about it for now. You mightn't believe this after what Zero just said, but we're your friends and comrades now… even Mr. Grumpy over there. So let's get going, okay?"

He smiled gently with an air of genuine affection. If Zero's ability was to pinpoint a person's greatest insecurities, then Agito's was to soothe and provide comfort.

Agito made his way towards the boat while Kira was already perched on the railing, having moved without Vincent noticing yet again.

Vincent closed his eyes for a moment and inhaled deeply. He held his breath for a few seconds in meditation, thinking back to the people of Ryuuga and the good he'd hoped to do for the community. He could feel his emotional state easing.

Zero watched patiently without a word. He had been standing on the beach waiting for everyone so he could push the boat free from the white dunes and embark.

Vincent opened his eyes slowly and exhaled through

a controlled breath. Surprisingly, he felt a little better and loaded himself onto the boat— moving past Zero without acknowledgment.

Zero pushed the boat free from the sand. It whirled to life in perfect unison with technology and mechanical prowess before speeding off into the distance over the endless ocean.

As the boat pulled away into the open waters, Agito pulled a tarpaulin canopy overhead and attached it from one end of the boat to the other—covering the four occupants almost entirely.

"The cloaking technology works best on stationary objects and closed vehicles. But this is an open-air boat, so this canopy reflects the sky and the ocean surrounding us and camouflages the boat. No sense in a secret base if everyone can see you coming and going, you know?" Agito helpfully informed.

***

Several hours passed, and a full moon hung high in the sky.

Vincent peered from beneath the canopy and stared

into the endless empty darkness.

"You asked how I got these scars," Agito said quietly.

After hours of traveling in awkward silence, Vincent jumped at the sound of his voice.

"I come from a massive city west of here called Brizden. It's about the size of the Ryuuga Metropolis, but it's one of the tech capitals of Kou. My father was head of the Noreaga Familia and extremely wealthy."

Vincent leaned closer, eager to hear more.

"Well, to tell you properly about my scars, there's a little world history you need to be aware of. Do you know what a relic is?" Agito asked.

Vincent shook his head as Agito fiddled with the pendant around his neck, rubbing the green crystal with his thumb.

"Relics are a product of 'the Golden Age'—a bygone era, in a time when magic was everywhere, and everyone could wield it. Records from back then are vague at best, but one thing we do know is that these relics were made to fight against a demonic horde that invaded about a thousand years ago. They attacked without warning and nearly wiped out the entire planet. Historians later called this 'The Rapture.' Anyway, these relics are wearable items infused with powerful magics, giving the wielder the ability to use all sorts of powers. To this day, we know very little about who the invading army was or where they came from. But it was their spilled, demonic blood upon the lands that gave rise to a terrible epidemic. A plague that infected and altered many lifeforms— twisting them into demented and foul creatures. This was known as *the Dark Calendar*."

Vincent became slack-jawed in disbelief.

"It was actually during the Dark Calendar that hellhounds were born or—created."

Vincent hadn't realized that he had been holding his breath. The shock on his face was all too clear to Agito, even in the moonlit darkness.

Agito smiled, enjoying Vincent's rapt attention.

"The Wood Wolf was once a calm and good-natured canine, but the plague changed their appearances and temperament and altered them from diurnal hunters to nocturnal creatures that could no longer stand the light.

This plague was but one of three near-extinction events during the time of the Dark Calendar. Millions perished, and the remaining relics were eventually scattered and lost throughout the world."

Agito was a born storyteller. Even Kira was completely still, pretending not to listen while secretly enjoying the tale. Vincent hung on every word.

Agito held his pendant to the moonlight, catching its dazzling green hue.

"Some relics are more powerful than others, and some were even able to manipulate the elements themselves. These are considered the rarest."

Agito ignited a small flame from the tip of his index finger.

"Would you put that thing out?!" Zero barked quietly, emerging from a dark corner and interrupting the mysterious atmosphere.

"Light can't be cloaked, and I'd rather not have our position compromised because you want to give this moron a history lesson!"

Agito rolled his eyes at Zero, but the flame vanished

instantly.

"You see, this relic is one of the most valuable in existence. It controls the element of fire. At some point during the Dark Calendar, the fire and lightning relics were subject to a military experiment, fusing them together. It would have given the user the ability to control *two* elements from the *one* relic. This, in turn, would have given rise to all sorts of powers being infused and stockpiled into destructive relics of unfathomable power."

Vincent gingerly touched the crystal, sliding his finger across the glassy surface.

"I'm guessing that it didn't work out then?" Vincent asked, looking up at Agito.

"Quite the opposite—they succeeded. The two elemental relics were fused, becoming a relic known as the Sunstorm Crystal. Unfortunately, the destructive power proved far too great, and it was eventually separated again, using the same alchemy that created it."

Vincent released the crystal.

He was struggling to keep track of all this new

information.

"What's alchemy?" he asked, ignoring a poorly covered laugh from Zero.

"As I mentioned before, thousands of years ago, all humans were born with magic," Agito explained while maintaining an air of mystery.

"From what the records show, society was entirely different back then. Over time, we evolved and developed science. Eventually, humans began combining scientific methods and formulas into the magics they cast. This gave birth to alchemy. It's said that we were able to do incredible things with alchemy. Things that were once thought impossible. We're not sure what happened, but humans lost the ability to cast magic at some point after the Rapture, and thus…alchemy was lost to us forever. That's also why we can't make new relics anymore either."

Vincent's eyes had glazed over.

"Right," he said weakly.

Agito smirked.

"I know this is a lot, but my story will bring you up to

speed on a lot of what you need to know. In fact, I think that's why I was one of the people sent to escort you."

"Oh yeah, and why was the cyclops sent? Just to piss me off?" Vincent quipped, flicking his head in Zero's direction.

"I was sent to kick your ass. Best assignment I've ever been given, too!" he chuckled, still looking straight ahead.

Agito cleared his throat.

"Anyway, my father was obsessed with the legend of the Sunstorm crystal. He used his wealth and power to research the origin of the two halves and managed to purchase the fire relic in a black-market bidding war." Agito hesitated, his face darkening.

"Then, when I was eleven, our estate was attacked."

Vincent's mind sharpened at this.

"It was the middle of the night, and I remember looking for my mother in all the chaos. When I finally found her, she was vaporized by someone wielding the lightning relic in front of my eyes. I couldn't see him well amidst the fires that were engulfing the room and burning through our home."

Agito was no longer looking at Vincent, and the words seemed to tumble from him as if he were replaying the events in his mind.

"Turns out, my father had prepared several evacuation plans in the event that we were attacked. So, I was rushed out by one of the maids through a secret tunnel that ran under the mansion grounds. The maid gave me the fire relic and had me run under the cover of darkness to one of my family's safehouses on the outskirts of town. I was the sole survivor.

Sadness overtook Agito's face.

"Seeing my mother die like that…it's one of the most vivid memories I have from my childhood, and it still haunts me to this day."

Agito trailed off, lost in thought.

Vincent was quiet, waiting patiently for Agito to continue and unsure how to respond.

"I lived in that safe house for seven years, raised in secret by an elderly woman who'd been secretly employed by my father for longer than I'd been alive.

She passed away when I was eighteen, and so I moved out…traveling on my own. For about a year and a half, I wandered aimlessly. I was aggressive and violent to everyone, and I was consumed with a thirst for vengeance. That is, until I met the director."

Agito's expression softened.

"I like to think that my scars from that night represent the family that I lost.

"My mother…and my father," he said, running his fingers down the cross-shaped scar on his cheek. And my older sister, Sophia," He tenderly touched the single slash across his left eye.

Vincent's stomach was churning. He was beside himself with grief for Agito. Loss and the need for vengeance were something he could understand all too well. As for family…he had lost his own mother and father to sickness when he was young—followed by his grandfather soon after that. He knew what it was like to be alone.

"I'm so sorry," Vincent whispered sadly.

Agito smiled.

"Thanks, but you don't need to be sorry. I carried the guilt of surviving for many years, and while I still want to find the man responsible, I'm no longer living for vengeance alone. I'm the sole survivor of the Noreaga's—despite the newspapers reporting that we all had died. I was entrusted this relic, and I'll carry it with pride each and every day that I draw breath. I'll find my family's murderer and bring them to justice…all the while, I'll become stronger while protecting the weak!"

Vincent found himself in awe of Agito. Never in his life had he met someone with such a calm yet unwavering resolve. It was something that he wished to emulate within himself.

"Terrible things happen to innocent people all the time," Agito continued. "And you'll find that everyone in our organization has their own tumultuous history. After all, you don't find yourself working for GRAVE if you've lived a comfortable life. But you'll also find that great strength can come from turmoil and adversity. Regardless, we've all come together to use our abilities for the sake of others. That's the reason you're here too,

Vincent. You can use your strength…not just for your own ambitions, but for the people of the world. I'm sure Zero at least mentioned that!"

Zero scoffed.

"Both of you quit your yammering and get some shut-eye. We should be arriving by sunrise, and you'll need all the rest you can get."

"Actually, I have a question, Zero," Vincent replied disobediently.

Zero didn't react, maintaining his gaze out onto the darkened horizon.

"Back when we fought, I remember standing in front of you. Then, you clicked your fingers, and the next thing I remember, I was waking up on the cliff's. What the hell happened?"

Agito let slip a laugh, louder than he intended.

"Awww you hit the poor guy with Trigger? That's pretty low, Zero" he chuckled.

Zero sighed deeply and looked back in Agito's direction.

"Yeah, but you've seen his attitude…he needed to be

taken down a peg or two."

"What's Trigger?" Vincent interjected.

Zero reluctantly looked over at Vincent—frustration clear on his face. He made little effort to hide that he found talking to Vincent a chore.

"Okay, you haven't started any fights in a few hours, so I guess I'll reward you with an answer." he belittled. "You know those blasts of light I hit you with?"

Vincent nodded in anticipation.

"Well, that's a spiritual energy attack. Think of it as my fighting spirit, given physical form.

"You mean like in the comics?" Vincent asked—his curiosity now filled with a child-like wonder.

Zero sat with his elbows on his knees, bowed his head, and smirked. "Yeah, pretty much. Although, I don't know what surprises me more…the fact that you understood my explanation, or that you actually get comic-books back in that dustbowl you call a home."

Zero lifted his head to assess Vincent's reaction.

Clearly, he was offended by this undeserved dig, but to Zero's astonishment, Vincent remained calm, so he continued.

"Look, all meisters can perform spiritual attacks, however, usually they do damage on contact with the target. Trigger is a move I especially developed...and it's a little different. You see, when I use this attack, I shoot energy blasts that I call 'sleepers' into the target. Rather than exploding on impact, they're absorbed into the person's body. I can control how much of my spiritual power that I want to put into each blast, but that power lies dormant within the target, until a time of my choosing. Usually, in the heat of battle, most *overconfident* opponents will either assume that I'm out of power, or just weak"

Vincent's body was tense, and he broke out in a cold sweat. His head dipped slightly ashamed that he had made both of these assumptions during their fight.

However, as he went to break eye contact; Zero leaned in closer, filling the sea air under the tarpaulin with murderous intent.

"I'll shoot a few into the poor sucker until I'm happy with the amount they've accumulated...and then," he then extended a single arm outward in Vincent's direction, "BANG!"

Zero snapped his fingers, making Vincent jump a little—unconsciously clutching at his chest.

"You're such a douchebag sometimes Zero, I swear." Agito judged harshly.

But despite Agito's provocation, Zero had a wicked gleam in his eye as he held Vincent's gaze.

"This is just the beginning, Vincent. Tomorrow…the real fun begins."

Zero

Jet

Agito

Kira

www.ingramcontent.com/pod-product-compliance
Lightning Source LLC
Chambersburg PA
CBHW070324130626
46556CB00007B/2717